I0655403

Love's Triple Play

Cascade Bay, Volume 3

Solara Gordon

Published by THE EARTH MOVED, LLC, 2022.

LOVE'S TRIPLE PLAY

First edition. July 7, 2022.

Copyright © 2022 Solara Gordon.

ISBN: 979-8986032504

Written by Solara Gordon.

Also by Solara Gordon

Cascade Bay
Love Reborn
Reunited By Choice
Love's Triple Play

Peyton Corners
Falling for You
Caught by Love's Slow Burn

Standalone
A Heart's Desire
To Love You Again
To Love You Again

Watch for more at https://solaragordon.com/.

Every story has its own pulse and flow. Ron, Mary and Jeff came to life on the page as they told me their story. I hope you enjoy their journey to their happily everafter.

Many thanks go out to:

-my street team and readers group *Solara's Glamorous Stars*

-my beloved life partner Jim Fleckenstein

-numerous polyamorous loves and friends-past and present

Here's to more stories and happy everafters from Cascade Bay!

Solara Gordon

July 2022

Chapter One

"*You're dating Ron Bailey?*" Jeff Nickerson asked, stepping back from Mary Bates. "When did that happen?"

Mary shook her head as she spoke. "Jeff, you can't expect things to be the same after being gone ten months."

"I didn't know my father would linger. Or that it would take four months to settle his estate." Jeff stepped back further until his back pressed against the office wall.

"No, you couldn't know. And you couldn't drop everything to come back when Ron offered to buy your third of the catering business." Mary pushed back from her desk. She rose and leaned forward, placing her hands on the desk. "Susan and Tim's decision to move to Sacramento caught me off guard, too."

"A whirlwind of shit happened. I guess the next question is, what about us?" Jeff asked, looking away again.

Jeff's gaze barely met hers since she told him about dating Ron. Mary pressed her lips together. Jeff hadn't asked for exclusivity before he left nor talked about it when they started seeing each other. He'd never officially asked her on a second date or introduced them as a couple.

She'd grown close to Ron. He knew she cared for Jeff. Ron helped her take care of her granddaughter along with his youngest sister's toddler. Jeff didn't know that her stepdaughter Darcey had moved back to Cascade Bay while he was settling his father's estate in Europe. Where did that leave her and Jeff?

Mary licked her lips and moved around her desk. She perched on the edge closest to Jeff. "Is there a me and you? We hadn't discussed that before you left."

"How more you and me can it get than sleeping together and spending time at each other's places?" Jeff moved toward her. His hazel eyes changed color like Susan's cat when he was pissed at you. It was like he cussed you out as they went from gold to green and back to blue.

"Talking about it. Having an agreement. Actually admitting you and I had second and third dates." Mary crossed her arms tight against her chest. "Assuming doesn't mean it's a fact."

She watched Jeff's chest rise and fall as he exhaled, letting go a long sigh. He reached up, running his fingers through his hair. How had she missed the subtle changes? His black hair curled in places she hadn't noticed before. He wore it longer than before he left. She caught her bottom lip between her teeth as he reached for the chair next to her. Could she admit she missed him? Did she dare say it without them talking things out?

Jeff dropped into the chair next to the desk. Doing the good son duty had come with a price. His estranged father's wanderlust had taken him on offbeat paths most of his life to the point of divorcing his first two wives. His final path took him to central Europe, where he'd met Ona, the last woman to settle him down. What possessed his father to have more children, Jeff didn't know. All that mattered now was Ona and his new younger siblings didn't have to worry about money or a roof over their heads like he had. The restaurants he advised Ona on buying started showing growing profits before he left. What he was going to do with his half-a-mill inheritance, he didn't know. He thought Mary would be part of it. Had he thought wrong?

"Guess I fucked up pretty badly. Would an apology help?" He slid lower in the chair and gripped the arms.

Mary's snorted laugh aimed hard for his gut and heart's vulnerable areas. If he gripped the arms harder, he'd crack the plastic. Maybe the pain and anguish churning deep in his belly would lessen if something distracted him. What would distract him? Mary was the one thing that kept him sane during his darker moments in Europe. Damn, he had messed up. His tunnel vision had kicked in and...he looked up. Mary watched him like a hawk sizing up the prey within its sight.

Mary smiled at him and unfolded her arms. A good sign? He wasn't guessing at anything. He repeated his earlier question. "Would an apology help?"

"There was a time when I thought I owed you one."

"You don't."

"Hear me out, please."

"Okay." He put his hands in his lap. Breaking Mary's chair wouldn't endear him to her any quicker if she were willing to forgive him.

"I thought a lot about what happened after you left. Asked myself if you owed me an apology. For a while, I thought maybe you did." Mary sat in the chair next to him.

"Your thoughts now?" Jeff sat up straighter, keeping Mary in his view. She wore her hair shorter. More than once, Ona had remarked on how pretty Mary's brunette hair and brown eyes were. He remembered her brown eyes, but hair color wasn't something he paid much attention to.

"We both shut up and waited for the other to make contact. You and I both are victims of circumstances we had little control over in many ways."

Jeff nodded. "Spot on. My blasted tunnel vision kicked in, and the rest is history." He looked down and up as he continued talking. "How about we both say sorry?"

Mary chuckled. He squirmed, rubbing his wet palms on his jeans. He took a deep breath and held it. He tried not to stiffen outwardly. Here came the no?

"It's scary how our thoughts run parallel sometimes." Mary leaned toward him, holding her hand out. "Before I say I'm sorry, I need you to know one thing."

"What's that?" He leaned forward, reaching for her hand.

Mary leaned closer, her fingers within reach of his. "I'm not giving up Ron."

Jeff dropped his hand. "You what?"

"I want to see both of you. You both intrigue me." Mary started to draw back.

Jeff stood up and moved to the right of the chair Mary sat in. "Trying to play Ron and me against each other?"

Mary rose. "No, not that at all. You each complement parts of me. Ron's a polyamorist. We've been talking about where we mesh."

"Have you slept with him?" Jeff folded his arms tight against him. God, talk about insecurities running rampant.

"I'm not answering that. This is about you and me. I asked you if there is an us. If you're interested, that includes me seeing Ron. Still open to saying I'm sorry to each other?" Mary laid her hand on his arm.

Jeff pressed his lips together. His ego screamed, *no, don't go there*. His heart whispered *you know you are*. And his Id, well, its horny lopsided smile just said getting laid was better than doing it alone. Not that he'd had time in the last week to think about that. Delayed overseas flights, canceled connections, and little to no sleep had grabbed his immediate attention. His internal clock kept pinging he should be asleep since it was the middle of the night in Europe.

He licked his lips and replied, "I'm sorry. I'm saying it 'cuz I am. I want to see you. I'd like to think there's an us."

He stopped and clapped his hand over his mouth, covering up another yawn. Coming straight from the airport wasn't such a great idea. Jet lag didn't cure itself by sleeping on the flight. He needed a decent night's sleep and food. He might make sense with a clearer head and rested and not come across as reactive. He dropped his hand and leaned down toward Mary. He pressed his lips to her forehead and drew back. He'd forgotten how much their five-inch difference in height made.

Mary reached up and patted his cheek. "I can see why you asked about an overnight. You really should have gone home and crashed."

"Probably. I dreamt about you many nights and being cuddled by you. I'd hoped tonight would be the first of many. I'm wrong." Jeff turned back to his chair and picked up his messenger bag.

Mary cleared her throat. "How about I drop by after Ron and I have dinner? I'm free until noon tomorrow."

Jeff slung his bag over his shoulder. He shrugged. "What about Ron? Don't you need to talk about you and me with him?"

Mary smiled and hugged him. "Good call. We've done a bit of that. Tonight, it sounds like you need me. Ron is picking up his niece after dinner with me. I don't think he's going to want to put the make on me."

"Sounds like our babysitting Susan and Tim's triplets or Nina and Leslie's twins." Jeff hugged Mary back, leaving his hand on her shoulder.

"Tabitha is one lively preschooler. At four and a half, she is talkative, energetic, and loves to learn." Mary stepped away from him and moved toward the door. "How about I call you when Ron and I are done with dinner?"

Jeff nodded as he made his way toward the office door. He stifled another yawn and blinked. "Sounds doable. I'm glad I've got a short drive to the condo."

He reached for Mary's hand as they stepped into the hall leading to the front of the floral shop. She entwined her fingers with his. He raised their joined hands to his lips and pressed a quick kiss along Mary's knuckles.

"Thanks. It's good to know you still care." Mary leaned closer, her lips puckered.

"Never stopped caring. Too many things demanding priority. I admit I messed up." Jeff brushed his lips over Mary's and let go of her hand. "I best get going. I've got one stop to make on the way."

Mary looked at him quizzically. He grinned. "You know how I hate to grocery shop. But I have to."

Mary chortled. "Go on home. I'll have Bev, my assistant, run by the store and drop things off for you."

Jeff waved as another yawn overcame him. He called out as he strode toward the door. "Got basic toiletries on me. You know what I eat. Need laundry stuff, too. Later."

He didn't dare look back. Mary's comments hit closer than he cared to admit. Truth didn't offer a choice between soft or rough. It came with a touch that could keep on gut-punching him or he could step back and decide where he went next. He could move forward, assessing where they stood and how Ron fit into the mix. There was staying mired in the past, not letting go of the crumbled and torn picture that didn't touch reality. One he'd built without taking time to examine building materials. Dreams and desire could build many things. Depending on the job, they could use help.

Jeff unlocked his car. The new car smell reached up and caressed his nostrils. The sports car purred as he started the engine—his first indulgence with his new funds. As he backed out of the parking space, one thing stood out in his mind. Ron, his business partner and college bestie, was close up and personal in ways they'd never been before. Sharing Mary was going to take getting used to if they went that route.

Mary stood in the shop door, watching Jeff drive away. She swallowed hard as she let go of the door handle. She'd bristled at his nonchalant entrance when he first arrived. His assumptive question came out like he expected her to be in the same position and doing the same thing from ten months ago. Once she'd gotten over the initial shock of seeing him in the flesh instead of on a computer screen half asleep due to time differences and continents between them, she'd regained her composure. Her heart skipped a beat with his first hug and then another. Yes, she'd fallen for him more than she realized.

Then there was Ron. The unexpected that snuck up on her and tugged at parts of her she'd forgotten about. Two unique men who had parts of her...Mary sighed. Possibly parts of her heart. Something she hadn't dared to acknowledge in quite a while. Were the three of them up to the challenge she'd issued? Find a way for the three of them to...shaking her head, Mary walked back to her office. She didn't know what to anticipate next.

She needed to talk to Ron. She picked up her cell phone and scrolled to his number. His photo and contact information came up. Ron's short-cropped ginger-red hair and blue eyes drew her from the moment she'd met him. Like Jeff had attracted her with his wit and infectious laugh and his cat-like hazel eyes. She pushed the call button.

Ron answered on the third ring. "Hi, Mary."

"Hey, Ron," she replied. "Good time to talk?"

"Sure. Last of the late lunch crowd just left." Ron leaned back against the booth he sat in. "What's up?"

"Jeff's back." Mary didn't say more.

Ron nodded. "I know. He texted me to pick him up at the train station."

"You knew and didn't say anything?" There was no mistaking the agitation in Mary's voice. Her edgy tone and higher pitch said it loud and clear.

"Dropped him at the dealership to pick up his new car. Not more than a ten-minute run from the station. Didn't leave time to talk." Ron sipped his coffee.

Mary's sigh came out of the phone as if she were next to him. He pressed his lips together. He knew that sigh. Five months of friendship and three months of dating put that particular sigh in front of him more than once. Its deep and heavy tone told of her frustrations. He'd stay quiet a few moments more. If she didn't speak, he'd ask his question.

"Okay," Mary said. "He came here. Acting like nothing between us changed."

Ron nodded again, setting his coffee mug down. He shouldered the phone as he turned in the booth, stretching his legs out on the seat. "I see."

Mary snorted. "Stop being nonchalant. Don't you care what I told him?"

Ron rolled his eyes heavenward. "I care to a point. Share what you want to."

"I told him about us."

"Okay."

"Is that all you can say?"

"I could say more and jump to conclusions. We both know that doesn't solve anything." Ron pulled his coffee mug to him. He grasped the mug and finished speaking. "We knew he'd be back at some point."

"Yes," Mary responded. "I guess I need to tell you something."

Ron chuckled. "I almost said okay. I think you deserve a better reply. How about 'go ahead'?"

Mary's laugh flowed out of the phone. She didn't sound very tense. "I told Jeff I want to see both of you."

Ron drank the rest of his coffee, grimacing at its coldness. He set the mug down and pushed it away. He took hold of the phone and swung his legs off the booth seat. "How'd he take it?"

"I'm not sure. He kept yawning and trying to sound like he got what I said."

"I'm good with you seeing Jeff. We've discussed this." Ron paused, waiting for Mary's response. When nothing came, he continued speaking. "Are we on for tonight?"

"Yes. After dinner, I'm going over to Jeff's."

Ron glanced at his watch as he replied. "Good. I need to finish what I'm doing here and head home. Pick you up around six?"

"Sounds good," Mary said. "Oh, there's one more thing."

Ron smiled and said, "Okay."

Mary laughed. "I may spend the night with Jeff."

"Sounds like you need to talk this one out. We can do that at dinner, okay?"

"Sounds great. See you around six," Mary said and hung up.

Ron laid his phone on the table. He pulled the day's receipts and the open laptop computer sitting next to them to him. The sooner he dropped the bank deposit in the night drop, he might get home quicker. Mary sounded like she wanted to take their relationship to the next level. A level that included Jeff. How was Jeff going to handle this? That added another aspect to everything.

Chapter Two

R on glanced at his watch. Six o'clock and he was stuck in traffic. Traffic hadn't moved for the last twenty minutes. Ten minutes earlier, three cop cars sped by with lights and sirens on full blast. Another siren sounded, followed by the blast of an air horn. He glanced in the rearview mirror. Two fire engines were making their way in and out of traffic to the highway's shoulder. Great, he wasn't going anywhere for a while longer. The bright spot in all this, his sister had canceled his babysitting. Poor Tabitha had the flu-like her older cousins, who she'd spent the day with. He wasn't getting near his sister or Tabitha until they were better.

What did he do while he sat in traffic and waited? He'd finished the audiobook he was listening to on the way to work. The local talk radio station did an all-news hour until seven. Listening to music didn't bolster him. He reached for his messenger bag lying on the passenger seat. As he took out his cell phone, it buzzed. He looked at the screen. It showed two text messages and a missed call from Jeff. It also displayed low battery warning. He plugged the car charger cord in and connected his phone.

The messages were from Mary. She was running late and stuck in traffic. Ron chuckled. Neither of them were going anywhere fast. Not that they had plans to do more than dinner. Still, he knew Mary felt the same way he did about being late. They didn't run their businesses that way. Punctual and plenty of time between appointments, flexing with their clients, and drawing the line when needed brought them repeat business and great word-of-mouth advertising. Susan had sold them her final portion of the business when Jeff left for Europe. His silent partner aspect had worked to a point. When the catering portion of the business grew to more than Jeff could handle from overseas, selling it made sense.

Ron held the phone to his ear as his voicemail started. "Hey dude," Jeff said in between yawns. "I wanna talk about you and Mary. I didn't know you're a polyamorist. We need to talk face-to-face. Lunch tomorrow, okay?"

As the message ended, Ron glanced in his rearview mirror. Two ambulances were barreling up the shoulder, lights flashing and intermittent sirens wailing. Great, he and traffic weren't going anywhere for a lot longer.

He scrolled through his contacts until he found Mary's number. She picked up on the third ring.

"Hey, your ears must be burning. We were just talking about you," Mary said.

"We?" Ron asked.

"Yes. Jeff and me. He called to let me know Bev just got to his place with the groceries he asked for."

"You running a side business I don't know about?" Ron asked, noticing the sunset out over the bay. "Crap, way things are going, we aren't going to get dinner."

Mary's snicker came through as though she was in the car with him. "Look, I got Jeff on the other line, let me conference him in. Before I do, I sent Bev to pick him up some groceries so he wasn't driving asleep at the wheel."

Ron held the phone away from him. Did he want to talk with Jeff and Mary at the same time? What kind of conversation would this be? Jeff's tone in his message sounded perturbed and out of sorts. If it got out of hand, cutting the call short was an option. Maybe a faceless phone discussion might ignite some talk that broke down barriers. Hell, he had some reservations, and he was the experienced one out of them. No one ever said polyamory was easy. It wasn't for the faint of heart either. He wet his lips and replied, "Sure, go ahead. We've got to start talking at some point."

"I know. Maybe the phone is the best place to start," Mary offered.

Ron chuckled. "I agree."

"You agree on what?" Jeff asked.

"How long have you been listening?" Ron retorted.

"Just added him," Mary countered. "Seriously."

Ron shook his head as traffic slowly moved forward. He shouldered his phone as he gripped the steering wheel. "Okay, give me a moment. I need to put you on Bluetooth before the cops decide I'm ticket fodder."

"Oh, shit," Mary replied. "I need to, as well."

"How about this," Ron offered. "I'm close to the exit for Jeff's place. We meet there?"

"This is turning into face-to-face," Mary responded.

Jeff's yawn came through the phone loud and clear. "Excuse me," he said. "I need ten minutes to shower and get decent."

"I can pick up a couple five-dollar pizzas." Ron held the phone away from him, pushed the speaker button, and laid the phone on the passenger seat. He glanced into the rearview mirror again, signaled, and moved on to the shoulder, easing his way into the line moving toward the exit.

"Pepperoni and ham if they got 'em," Mary answered. "I need to get gas before I come over. I'll pick up some salad and sodas."

"Sounds good," Jeff added. "That gives me twenty minutes to shower and dress. Another ten to stuff odds and ends in the closet."

Mary's laughter rang out. "At least make room for us to sit and be comfortable."

"Look, I unwrapped what furniture I could before dropping on the bed rolled up in a blanket to nap." Jeff blew a raspberry into the phone and hung up.

Ron smiled as he exited the highway. This wasn't the evening he envisioned. Nor was the conversation he just had either. Life brought surprises and challenges. How this turned out wasn't predictable. Right now, he had pizza to pick up.

"You still there?" Mary asked.

"Yes," he replied, turning at the next light. "You okay with this?"

Mary's sighed and answered. "Confused and unsure."

"I understand. I think we all are." Ron turned into the parking lot of Pizza Haus. "We're hungry. Once we've eaten and broken the ice in person, things may ease up."

"I hope so. I'd hate to have to choose between either of you," Mary said and ended the call.

Ron turned his car off and got out. He stuffed his phone in his pants pocket as he entered the restaurant. Doubt floated below the surface for the three of them. He understood that from negotiating boundaries and relationships with other polys. This time he was dealing with newbies. That took a different approach. One that moved as slow as any needed and lots of communication.

He approached the counter preoccupied with his thoughts. He looked down from viewing the order board to catch the server smiling and watching him. After a few minutes perusing the board, he placed his order—two pepperoni and ham pizzas and a large dessert brownie pizza

"How long before the order is ready?" he asked the server as he'd paid.

"Five to ten minutes. Have a seat." The server pointed to the row of chairs near the door. He sat on the one closest to him and resumed his earlier thoughts.

Mary had met several of his poly friends over the last two months. She had a basic understanding of what polyamory was about. What Jeff knew he couldn't say. How this first conversation would turn out, he wasn't sure. He didn't want to lose friends or the connection he and Mary had. How did he start the conversation? Maybe he let Jeff and Mary start it. Let them ask the questions and voice their concerns.

Ron drummed his fingers against his leg. Was he ready to admit his last poly relationship was more than a year ago? Even then, that one had been a flash that lasted six months until Lydia moved to Australia. Her job promotion had turned into an offer she couldn't turn down—double her mid-thirties salary and a house rent-free for two years. Last he heard from her, she was dating an Aussie poly couple. His last serious relationship...well, if he was honest with himself, it was probably over two years ago. Madeline's deployed husband had given them his blessing before he deployed. Dan's next duty station offered a chance for a house and a permanent place for them to live since he was a year out from retirement. Even with an open invitation to visit Dan and Madeline, Buffalo, NY, didn't hold the enticement like other places where snow wasn't a four-letter word.

Now there was Mary. Ron sighed. Yes, a primary relationship was what he wanted. Would that come about with Mary?

He glanced at the counter. The server approached with his order.

"Here you go, sir. Anything else?" She set two pizza boxes on the counter along with a large plastic bag.

Ron peered inside the bag. He could make out part of the label on the box on the bottom. It held the brownie. On top of the box lay three Styrofoam plates, a stack of napkins and cutlery in plastic packets. "No. Looks good. Thanks!"

As he turned away, the server said, "Valerie says enjoy and good to see you again."

Ron leaned to his left and caught sight of Valerie, the owner. Ron waved and called out. "Thanks! Good to see you, too."

A soft wind blew as he opened the door and exited. Fresh pizza wafted up, teasing his nose. He inhaled, savored the fragrance, and hurried to his car. His stomach growled as he set the pizzas and bag on the back seat. He hoped traffic had eased allowing him to get to Jeff's quickly. If he had to sit in traffic again—he wasn't waiting to sample a slice.

Two easy turns thanks to green arrows in his favor and he eased into traffic on Lake Road Parkway. Jeff's condo complex sat close to the inland group of lakes at the outer edge of Cascade Bay's growing city limits. The city council had plans for three new schools, another development of houses, and an extension of the business corridor running out along the municipal airport road.

Since Leslie and Nina were living in Washington, D.C., due to Leslie's election to the House of Representatives, Tim and Susan's move to Sacramento left Mary and him running the party planning business.

Making new business connections and growing his portion of the business brought he and Mary together tighter than if he'd just run the diner. How were the three of them going to handle being in business and a relationship together?

Ron let out a deep pent-up sigh as he moved into the lane to turn into Bay Lakes, Jeff's condo complex. The light turned red as he reached the head of the lane. He kept one eye on the traffic light and glanced at the sunset out over the bay. Reds mixed with pinks and golds as the sun sunk lower in the sky. A few birds chirped as the sun disappeared from view.

Honk! Honk! Ron jumped. He looked in the rearview mirror. Mary sat behind him, waiting to make the turn like him. He turned onto the two-lane road leading to the completed condo buildings. The two lanes threaded their way between the six three-story buildings' parking areas. The last building closest to the clubhouse and pool area housed Jeff's condo.

As Ron parked, he could make out the surveying stakes that marked the far side boundary of the fifty-acre development. It looked like they marked off single-family home plots. Across the road from them, partially constructed townhomes and duplexes lined the dirt road leading to the construction area. Mary pulled into the parking space next to him. She waved as he got out of the car. He blew her a kiss as he made his way to the driver's side rear door. He reached in and picked up the two pizza boxes.

He placed the boxes on the roof of his car and leaned back in to get the bag when a hand fondled his ass. He tried to straighten up and see who dared such a PDA. *Thwack.* He banged up against the open car door.

"Ah shit," he cursed, dropping the bag on the seat. The brownie box inside slid out. He leaned in, grabbing at the box as he placed his hand on the seat to steady himself. Sounds of plastic crumpling followed by more cussing. He grabbed the bag in one hand and gave into the fall, landing on the seat, the box close to his open hand. Ron laid his hand on the box and slid it to him. He let go of the bag, letting it fall to the floor of the car. He put both hands on the seat and pushed upward to straighten up. *Thump!* He banged his head on the doorframe of the car and stumbled backward.

"Damn it, who the hell do you think..." He rubbed his head as he backed up. Ron looked over his shoulder, rolled his eyes, and sighed.

Mary gave him a weak grin and said, "Sorry. I didn't think I'd caught you off guard."

Ron walked back to the car, leaned in, snatched the bag off the floor, and stuffed the box in it. He ducked his head as he straightened. He backed up and held the bag out to Mary. "I think you can give me a hand with this."

Mary took the bag and apologized again. "Seriously, I'm sorry. Really sorry."

Ron moved closer to Mary. He leaned in and brushed his lips over hers. "Don't sweat it. Just don't come up behind me like that again, okay?"

"Yes," Mary said, taking the bag from him. "You could walk up behind my dad and he'd goose from you standing there."

"Understood. I punch, then punch again."

"Damn, you could have told me about this," Mary said, backing away from him.

Ron held up his hands. "Stop. Hear me out, okay?"

Mary nodded.

"You've never caught me off guard in close quarters before. I learned hard and fast that bullies don't back down until you show them you fight back."

"Wow. I'm glad you told me." Mary moved up beside him and puckered her lips.

Ron closed the distance between them and pressed his lips tight against hers. He moved back, creating space between them. "My old man walked out on my mom when I was seven. The cook at the restaurant she worked at took me under his wing and taught me the fine art of blacking an eye or two on a makeshift dummy in the back of the kitchen."

"I bet your mom wasn't happy about that," Mary said as he closed the doors and locked them with his keyless remote.

"She was glad Ian took an interest in me. Kept me out of trouble and away from the gangs." Ron retrieved the pizza boxes from on top of the car.

He faced Mary and winked. "Ian and Mom married a couple of years later. He adopted me right before Syndy was born. Moved all of us from Chicago to Sacramento."

"Ian sounds like a good man. Glad your mom and he got together."

Ron walked toward Mary's car. "Quite a few good years together. They like their retired life in Phoenix."

"Why hadn't you shared this before?" Mary asked.

"Hadn't given it much thought until now. I usually bring it up once the person I'm seeing and I get serious."

"How do you know you're getting serious?" Mary stopped by her car, setting her purse and bags on the trunk.

"Usually when we start sleeping together," Ron tossed out, moving up by Mary. "Or they ask about my personal life like our discussions have turned to recently."

"Wait," Mary called out as she got the bags holding a six-pack of soda and the salad and dressing from her car.

Ron stopped and turned. Mary put her purse over her shoulder and picked up the bags off her car. She trotted to where he stood. "What?" he asked as Mary's gaze met his.

"Are you saying we've gotten serious?" She didn't look away.

He shifted the pizza boxes to one side, leaned toward Mary, and said, "Yes. Otherwise, I wouldn't be here."

Chapter Three

Mary blinked, pressed her lips together, and nodded. Talk about catching someone off-guard. Ron definitely had. He hadn't said anything about them being a couple. Nor had he...she inhaled sharply. She hadn't said anything either. Some days, they spent hours together working on business items. Others, they talked on the phone briefly and a few went by without either of them contacting the other. Well, now the declaration was out.

Ron pulled back and pointed toward the building closest to them. "Jeff is waiting for us. I'm hungry. I bet you and he are, too."

She nodded again and started toward the building. Ron walked beside her. Halfway up the front walk, he entwined his fingers with hers. He raised their joined hands up to where they both could see them as they walked.

"I'm not competing with Jeff. We're business partners and friends regardless of the outcome of this evening." Ron started to lower their hands.

Mary stopped and faced Ron. "I don't know all Jeff's thoughts. He and I have things to work out. I didn't realize how much I still cared until we were face-to-face again."

"History can do that to people. If the good you had outweighs the rough spots, you want to recapture that essence. Not a bad thing." Ron lifted her hand to his lips and brushed them over her knuckles.

They continued walking toward the double glass door entrance. Mary held back as they waited for a couple to exit. She glanced at Ron and spoke. "I want to know something before we go in."

"Sure. Go ahead,"

"Do you desire me?"

Ron moved in front of her, touched her cheek, and replied. "Yes. I have for a while. I wanted to be sure you returned the feelings."

"Thanks," Mary responded. "I wasn't sure."

Ron smiled. "I understand. We need to talk about this at another point. Yes?"

"I agree. Tonight is about three. I'm nervous." Mary reached for the door and glanced at Ron. "I don't want to lose either of you."

Ron pulled the door open and moved aside to let her enter first. "You aren't losing me. Remember what I just said about friends and business partners?"

"Yes. I guess I'm looking for solid reassurance." Mary shook her head and entered the building. Both Jeff and Ron had waited before pursuing her. Jeff had come into the shop as a client before they started talking and getting to know each other. He'd sat and ate with her during one of her lunch breaks. That led to a dinner out and other get-togethers, his word not hers, before he'd kissed her and she reciprocated. Ron kissed her on the cheek and hugged her after they'd gone out. Today was the first he kissed her on the lips. He did check on their communication, making sure they were both on the same page, to quote him.

"I can't give you a guarantee. Or reassure you more. It's up to you to decide if I'm telling the truth or not," Ron said, entering behind her.

Mary inhaled, held her breath, and exhaled. She repeated the calming technique her grief therapist taught her after Warren died. Despite their fifteen-year age difference, Warren had encouraged her to explore and learn. He told her more than once life came with no set agenda, nothing pre-planned, and no road map. It was up to her to make her own path and follow what was right for her. Trust her gut and heart, he advised her repeatedly. It wasn't always easy and the paths she sometimes chose led to dead ends. The experience taught her to apply the lessons learned and move on.

"True. I appreciate your honesty. It's one of the reasons we get along well." Mary made her way across the lobby toward the elevator. As Ron caught up with her, she added, "Thanks for being you."

"You're welcome. Anything less would be a lie. I can't fake me."

Mary chortled. "I certainly can't imitate you either. I can't sing in that deep baritone voice you've got."

Ron grinned at her and stuck out his tongue. Mary pressed her lips together, biting back where her thoughts went. She grinned and said, "Ah well, someday maybe you'll sing me to sleep the way you do Tabitha."

"Ask me to stay over and you might get your own special lullaby," Ron offered.

Mary ducked her head, walked to the elevator, pushed the call button, and looked back at Ron. He made a semi-bow and walked up to her. He leaned down and whispered close to her ear, "Might also get you to sing out a pleasing orgasm song."

She licked her lips, glanced at Ron, and said, "You gotta wanna first. Then see if your piccolo can reach those high notes."

Ron snorted as the elevator doors opened. He straightened up, shaking his head. He waited until they were inside to respond to her. "Good comeback, dear. I plan on making you reach those high notes again and again after a few auditions."

"What auditions?"

"Oh, you didn't know I adore multiorgasmic women?"

Mary pushed the button for the third floor. She fanned herself as she faced Ron. "This multiorgasmic woman might just wear you out."

"I do love a challenge," Ron quipped as they reached their floor.

Mary rose on her tiptoes and kissed Ron's cheek. "Thanks for helping me relax. You sure can flirt."

Ron smiled, winked, and walked out of the elevator humming. As she caught up with him, he stopped part way down the hall and remarked, "Maybe I wasn't flirting."

Mary opened her mouth, ready to zing another cheeky reply when a door close to them opened, and Jeff walked out, carrying a bulging trash bag. Jeff smiled and nodded as he walked past them, saying, "Trash receptacle needs to eat, too. Go on in."

Ron snickered, wet one fingertip, and drew a vertical line in the air. He murmured as they entered Jeff's condo. "Oh, you poor thing. Two men with similar senses of humor."

Mary gawked at Ron as she entered Jeff's condo. Similar senses of humor? Huh? What had she missed? "What are you talking about?"

"Inanimate objects treated like they're alive." Ron placed the pizzas on the pass-through counter. "Like me and the blender? Or my mulish computer?"

Mary smiled and nodded. "Can relate. I got a few of those dang things, too."

Ron chuckled. "One item we all have in common."

"What's that?" Jeff asked, closing the door behind him.

"Quirky sense of humor," Mary added.

Jeff grinned at her and faced Ron. "Is that what you were going to say?"

"Yes," Ron said, walking over to her. He reached for the bags she held. "I think there's another thing we all have in common."

Mary looked at Jeff. He shrugged and shook his head. She handed Ron the bags. "Okay, what is it?"

"We care for each other, and we're friends." Ron set the bags on the counter next to the pizzas.

"I agree," Jeff said, walking into the kitchen. "Nice to have things to build upon."

"Build upon?" Mary asked, following him into the kitchen.

"Yes. Did a bit of research before I fell asleep." Jeff crossed the kitchen to the refrigerator and turned. "Seems multipartnered relationships often have a common ground to build upon."

"Whoa," Ron said. He leaned against the doorframe, his arms at his sides. Jeff glanced at Ron's hands. They appeared opened and relaxed. Good, starting a fistfight wasn't what he had in mind. Food and discussion were as far as he got in possibilities for the evening.

Ron stepped into the kitchen. "There's a lot of research out there. Some of it's based on factual findings. Some on conjecture. Be careful what you believe."

"Good point," Jeff replied. "I remember Mrs. Markham's literature class and the citations we had to come up with."

"Lord," Ron groaned. "That woman would hound you on authenticating your findings four times over."

"Mrs. Markham?" Mary asked, opening and closing cabinets.

"Yes, junior year American lit class. What are you looking for?" Jeff inquired.

"Glasses. Makes putting ice and soda together easier, you know."

"My bad. I haven't unpacked them yet." He walked over to the box closest to the sink and back wall of cabinets, tore the box open, and sat three glasses in the sink.

"Did you order everything and have it delivered?" Mary asked, squirting dish detergent onto the sponge in the sink.

"No. Movers packed up my old place and put stuff into storage about four months ago. Susan oversaw that for me. She called the people who helped her and Tim move." Jeff rinsed and dried each glass.

"I'm hungry. Let's get food on the table, and we can talk more then, okay?" Ron was at the stove with the oven open. "It'll take about five minutes to warm up the pizzas."

"I'll take care of the salad," Mary said, taking the bowl Jeff held out to her.

"I'll set the table." Jeff started back across the kitchen toward the pile of boxes he'd gotten the glasses out of.

"One of the bags has plates, napkins, and utensils. Why not use them?" Ron asked, placing one of the pizzas in the oven.

Jeff emptied the bags on the table, laid out plates, napkins, and packaged utensils. "Oh, double chocolate brownie. Thanks, dude. Haven't had one in a while."

"You're welcome." Ron set the other pizza on top of the stove. "I'll warm the other if needed."

"Hey, cold pizza for breakfast is good," Jeff added, laying the plastic bags on the sink counter.

"You have a microwave," Mary said, passing him. "You could warm it up."

"Nah," Ron countered. "Cold pizza and flat beer. The breakfast of culinary school graduates."

Jeff started laughing. "How many lectures did we get over that?"

"Let me think about that for a—" The oven time rang, cutting Ron off.

"Can we eat without all the reminiscing?" Mary asked, carrying the salad to the table.

"Pfft," Jeff started, and Ron joined him. Both did it again as she turned from the table with the plates in her hand.

She walked over to Jeff, pressed her lips against his and stuck her tongue out enough to touch his. He moved closer and wrapped his arm around her waist. His tongue dueled with hers briefly before he pulled away. He smiled and reached for the plates.

"Uhmm—no," she said and turned to face Ron, who gawked at them. She closed the space between her and Ron. She stopped when they were toe-to-toe. "Wouldn't want you to feel left out."

Mary leaned in and pressed her lips against Ron's. She traced his lips with her tongue. Ron opened his mouth and proceeded to give her a short passionate French kiss. His hand lay on her hip, steadying her as she broke the kiss. Ron murmured softly as she stepped back, "Remember, your special lullaby is ready when you are."

Mary fanned herself with the plates and glanced back at Jeff, who watched Ron and her. Her gaze met Ron's again. He nodded, kissed her cheek, and softly said, "You've declared your intentions. Both Jeff and I."

She wet her lips. "Yes, I did."

"You okay with that?" Ron asked, taking the plates from her.

"Must be or I wouldn't have kissed both of you."

Ron handed her two plates with pizza on them. "It's okay if you're not. Sometimes we catch ourselves off-guard. Don't sweat it."

Mary nodded briefly and turned away. She observed Jeff. He raised a hand, waved, then turned away, muttering something she couldn't make out.

Ron nudged her. "Let him be. We'll talk about it at the table."

Mary placed the plates on the table and took the third one from Ron. "Guess we all got caught off-guard."

"Could be. Let Jeff bring it up," Ron said, sitting down. "Sometimes the hardest part of poly isn't knowing your sweetie cares for another. It's the open affection and seeing it that knee-jerks you."

"Shit, I don't want to hurt Jeff." Mary sat down opposite Ron. "Or you."

"I'm not. You expressed your feelings openly, and that's good." Ron glanced over his shoulder. "Jeff, pizza's on. Ready to join us?"

"Yes, give me a minute. Need to wash my hands." Jeff went to the sink and turned the water on.

Mary looked at Ron, who shook his head and pointed to the salad bowl. "You want some?"

"Yes, thank you." Mary served herself and passed the bowl to Ron. He took some and sat the bowl next to Jeff's plate. She picked up her fork and began eating.

Jeff washed his hands twice. He'd clenched them tight to the point of fisting them as Mary kissed Ron. His first reaction had smacked him upside the head. They were kissing like she and he just had. The passion oozed off them and flooded the room as if the two of them were...

He took another breath and reached for a paper towel. They'd shared a hug and a kiss. Nothing more than Mary shared with him. What made it different? Why did he feel gut-punched? It wasn't like he didn't know about them. Or did he?

Get a hold of yourself, his conscience chided him. *It's not like they had sex in front of you. Are you or aren't you open-minded?*

He dried his hands, counted to five, and turned. Ron and Mary sat at the table calmly eating. A plate with pizza and a glass of ice with a soda can next to it marked his place. A spot for him to join them and be included. Or he could exclude himself, create a scene, destroy a friendship, and lose Mary altogether. As he tossed the paper towel in the trash, something he read in his quick internet search on polyamory came to mind. Communicate, communicate, and communicate again. Every comment said rough spots needed discussion. Okay, he needed to talk about how he felt.

He walked over to the table, sat down, and spoke. "Thanks, Ron, for getting the pizza. Thanks, Mary, for taking care of the salad and sodas."

"You're welcome," Mary and Ron each responded.

"However," Jeff began, picking up his slice of pizza. "Can we keep the PDAs to a minimum? I'm still digesting what I read and getting back on west coast time."

Ron held up his glass. "I agree. We need to respect everyone's feelings. We go as slow as any of us needs."

Mary picked up her glass and added, "I caught me off guard if it helps. I agree. Okay?"

Jeff set his pizza down and reached for his glass. "I'm in. Let me get a bit of this down me before we start talking."

He raised his glass, tapped it against theirs, and set it back on the table. He caught Ron and Mary's nods as he bit into his slice of pizza. Several quiet moments passed as they ate. Jeff reminded himself to chew more than once. No one was rushing him to taste a dish or hurry to another meeting. He was back in Cascade Bay. Home turf and his time were his. He filled his plate with salad and glanced at Mary. She met his gaze and smiled.

Jeff picked up his napkin, wiped his mouth, and voiced the question he kept coming back to. "Ron, why polyamory?"

"Good question. I'm hardwired this way." Ron held his slice of pizza up. "I see myself as part of a larger whole that interconnects. Like this slice is part of the pizza."

"Hardwired?" Mary laid her fork down. "Please explain."

"It's like preferences and tastes. You have certain foods and things you like. For me, it's polyamory. Monogamy doesn't feel right to me."

"Have you tried it?" Jeff asked in between bites of salad.

"A few times," Ron replied, standing. "Does anyone want more pizza?"

"Two pieces were enough for me." Mary started stacking the empty plates.

Jeff held up a finger, finished chewing and swallowed. "No more for me. Maybe later, though."

Ron chuckled. "Okay, I'll put the other one in the fridge. Keep talking."

"Did you become poly because monogamy didn't work for you?" Mary pushed back from the table.

"Partly. Saw too many of my friends getting angsted-up while dating and acting like they owned someone." Ron closed the fridge door.

Jeff wiped his mouth and asked, "Was I one of them?"

Chapter Four

"Let's continue this in the living room." Ron picked up his glass and napkin, grabbed another can of soda off the counter, and entered the living room. He sat down on the couch, setting his glass and soda on the end table.

Jeff sat in the chair across from him. Mary sat on the other end of the couch with her legs curled up.

Ron opened his soda and refilled his glass. He leaned back against the back cushion and picked up the thread of their conversation. "Jeff, you asked if you were one of the people I saw acting possessive or angsted-up."

"Yeah." Jeff nibbled on a piece of pizza crust.

"Never possessive to my knowledge. Angsted-up, yes. I've even gotten that way." Ron sipped his soda.

"What makes you polyamorous?" Mary asked.

"I'm curious, too," Jeff added.

"I've never expected one person to meet all my needs."

"Huh?" Jeff asked, sitting forward. "I don't get it."

"Let me explain it this way. You're a foodie, right? A chef who knows how to prepare many different dishes, yes?" Ron set his glass down.

"Well, yeah. You are, too." Jeff rested his elbows on his knees.

"Right. I like different cuisines. I prefer two or three as my mainstay. Same way I prefer my relationships. No single one meets my taste preference."

"This is why I have two to three pints of ice cream in my freezer and a wide variety of flowers in the shop," Mary said, drinking more of her soda.

"Correct," Ron said, sitting up more. "It boils down to I don't expect one person to meet all my needs."

Jeff placed his hands on his knees and asked, "How do you deal with jealousy?"

"I own it when I'm aware of it. Sometimes it blind-sides you. A couple I'm friends with label their jealousy 'foreign film.' Others have their own set of rules."

"Poly sounds like a lot of rules and regs. Bob, Carol, and Alice didn't seem to have that many." Mary stretched her legs out, sat up, and set her glass on the coffee table.

"It can be if that's what works for those in the relationship. Bob, Carol, and Alice started with a tight set of rules. They've changed as their triad aged."

"Triad?" Jeff asked.

"A group of three people who form a relationship or family unit. It can be open allowing outside relationships, or closed."

"Damn, there's a lot of shit to remember," Jeff fussed.

Ron chuckled. "It can be if you're trying to memorize it. There's no test or grade. Errors can and do occur."

"Why poly?" Jeff asked again. "I mean, it's not like you don't have gals hitting on you."

"True," Ron responded. "Think about it this way. You and I are friends. We're both interested in Mary."

"Yeah. So what?"

"Well, why should either of us lose out? If Mary likes or wants both of us, why choose?"

"You know," Mary spoke up, "I like a win-win proposition."

Jeff glanced at Mary. "You're sure about this?"

"Yes, I guess," Mary answered.

"You guess?" Ron questioned.

"Is any of this a certainty?" Mary shrugged. "I'm attracted to both of you. Don't want to lose either."

"How about this?" Ron offered. "We're embarking on an us." He pointed at each of them.

Jeff pressed his lips together and looked away. Relationships didn't come with guidebooks or most rules written down. Was this what Ona was talking about when she talked about his father's vagabond lifestyle, embracing her and their children, permitting them to experience different cultures, other countries and ways of life for a few months on up to a year? Jeff looked up. Ron and Mary watched him. Could he readily agree to an us that included the three of them?

Commit to a concept he still didn't completely grasp? He was damn sure about one thing. He wasn't getting it on with Ron.

Jeff held up his hand. "I'm certain I don't know what I'm getting into. There was a lot of stuff about threesomes and sex on my initial internet search. *I'm not into guys. Not going there.*"

"Neither am I. You're safe," Ron responded. "Threesomes aren't an expectation. Some like them. Others don't. Poly can include sex. We'll figure out what works for us."

Mary picked up her glass, shook it, rattling the remaining ice. She set it back down. "I don't get threesomes. Never got juiced by x-rated movies or the idea of watching others get it on."

"Maybe it's a guy thing," Jeff offered, shrugging as she looked at him.

"I don't think so," Ron countered. "I know men and women who enjoy them. Gets their hormones juicy."

"Does it get either of you juicy?" Mary asked, glancing at both of them.

"I get turned on by some. My want and need ignite together. Straight testosterone pumping through the body." Ron looked at Mary. "Kinda like when you get that jolt of chemistry when someone attractive catches your eye."

"I know that feeling," Jeff muttered.

Mary turned around, facing Jeff. "Oh? You do?"

"What do you think happened when I saw you? You jolted me and still do." Jeff nodded.

Mary shrugged. She'd keep her thoughts to herself. Offering opinions wasn't always a good thing.

Ron coughed, drawing Mary out of her thoughts. He smiled and said, "Don't worry about it. Attraction is part of why we're here. I think we agree that threesomes aren't happening."

"Yes," Mary answered.

"Same here," Jeff replied.

"That leads me back to my question. How about we embark on an us?" Ron pointed at each of them again.

Jeff tapped his lip, nodded, and spoke. "I'll try it. Are we making things up as we go along?"

"Some say there's guidelines. Others call 'em rules. Often you get info and decide what works for you." Ron drank more of his soda and turned to Mary. "How you doing?"

"Trying to digest all this and acknowledge my feelings." Mary stretched and yawned. "Excuse me."

Jeff put his hand over his mouth, yawning behind it. He glanced at his watch. Nine p.m. He and Mary were tired. He didn't know about Ron. He used to run on five to six hours of sleep during culinary school. Arching his shoulders, Jeff said, "How about divvying up the brownie and calling it a night? I'm beat."

Ron nodded and rose. "We've talked basics. Overload's easy with new concepts."

Jeff followed Ron into the kitchen. "I asked Mary to spend the night."

"Yes. She told me. I'm fine with it." Ron cut the brownie into thirds. "Got anything to put this in?"

Jeff opened the drawer closest to him and pulled out a gallon freezer storage bag. "Need more than one?"

"Yes," Ron said, taking the first from him. "Two more, please."

"Seriously, dude," Jeff began, holding out two more bags. "You're really okay with Mary staying with me tonight? Sex might happen."

Ron took the bags and faced him. "Okay with you and Mary is part of the equation. Sex—well, it's gotta be safe sex."

"I ain't kinky," Jeff quipped, taking one sealed bag from Ron.

"I know that," Ron said, laying the two remaining sealed bags on the counter. "I'm talking safe sex practices. Condoms, STD talks, prior partner exposure, and overall health."

Jeff swallowed hard. Admitting damn near ten months of celibacy didn't do much for a guy's ego. Health checkup was overdue. And STD tests...well, he and Mary weren't using condoms before he left. Did he tell all of this to Ron without Mary present or wait? Had Ron and Mary slept together? Were they practicing safe sex?

"Same needs to be asked of you." Jeff picked up the two other bags and put them in the refrigerator.

"True," Ron replied, washing off the knife he used and wiping down the counter with a wet paper towel. "I think Mary needs to be in on this. It involves her, too."

"What involves me?" Mary asked, walking into the kitchen.

Ron walked over to Mary, slid his arm around her waist, and answered, "Safe sex and you sleeping with Jeff tonight."

"Wow," Mary said, pushing away from him. "How did I become the hot topic again?"

"I brought it up," Jeff said.

"Is this about one-upmanship? Who gets to possess me?" Mary asked in a sarcastic tone, wrapping her arms tightly around her. She walked away from him and Jeff.

"Uhmm," Jeff began.

Ron held up his hand. "Let me. I started this part of the conversation."

Jeff nodded and leaned back against the counter. "Go ahead."

"Thanks." Ron faced Mary. "Jeff asked if I'm okay with you staying tonight and having sex."

"I hear you."

"I said being okay with you and him is part of the equation. Sex for me needs to include safe sex practices. You're part of the discussion. I said we need to include you."

Mary turned away from him. "And you, Jeff?"

Jeff looked away. Mary glanced at both of them. Ron blinked and took a couple of breaths. "Do we want to continue this in here or sitting in the living room?"

"I could use some water," Mary said, moving to the sink.

"I think we all could," Jeff said, setting three clean glasses on the counter.

Ron closed the distance between them. Someone had to start the new topic. Guess it might as well be him. He took the glass Jeff held out. "Thanks."

After drinking a couple of swallows, Ron spoke. "I've got nothing to hide from either of you. I'm not seeing anyone currently other than Mary. I hoped to be friends with benefits."

"Now you want more?" Mary asked.

"If things work out that way, yes." Ron faced Jeff. "I know you and Mary have history. I get you want her, too."

"What are you saying?" Jeff walked over to the kitchen table, pulled a chair out, and sat down.

"I'm STD-free. Last health checkup and STD tests were a month ago. Every partner I've been with, I used condoms for intercourse. Fluid bonded over oral sex." Ron sat down next to Jeff. He pulled out a chair and patted the seat. "Come on and join the discussion, Mary."

Mary set her glass in the sink and joined them. "I see the topic is sex. Not sure how that came to be. I'll toss my feelings in."

Jeff flashed a sheepish grin and nodded. Ron resisted the urge to roll his eyes. After all, everyone was entitled to their reactions. If they could take this from reacting to acting, then maybe they could have this last discussion and call it a night.

"Please share," Ron said, turning toward Mary. "I want to hear what you have to say."

Mary took a deep breath, glanced at Ron and Jeff, and said, "Jeff and I stopped having sex two months before he left. I had my annual physical and gyn checkup. STD tests, too."

"Have you had sex with anyone during Jeff's absence? I know we haven't gotten to that point yet." Ron laid his hand on the table, palm down. She knew that sign. He'd done it the first time they'd talked in depth. He wanted her to come to her own conclusions. He said a palm up was a peace offering. Sometimes peace came with a price. He didn't want her paying a price she wasn't willing to spend.

"Other than my toys—no. Replaced a couple of worn-out vibrators. Of course, I'm not saying where my fantasies went during those moments." Mary looked at Jeff and continued speaking. "No health issues. STD free too."

Jeff's gaze met hers. He briefly nodded and laid his hand near Ron's, palm down, as well.

Jeff cleared his throat. "Guess it's my turn, now."

Mary and Ron nodded almost simultaneously. Jeff licked his lips and began talking. "I got checked out while in Europe. Ona and my younger brothers came down with the flu. Doctor checked me out to be sure I didn't have it."

"Good," Ron said. "What about STDs and your overall sexual health?"

"Got a complete physical before I left ten months ago. I was tired and agitated. Even sought some sort of counseling. STD test came back clear. Is that enough?"

"I think so," Ron responded. "Mary, what do you think?"

Mary laid her hand palm down on the table. "I'm going to suggest we call it an evening. I feel safe enough to have sex with either of you right now. Let's just play it by ear for the next few days."

Ron laid his hand on top of hers. Jeff followed suit.

"By ear may not work," Ron offered. "I'm willing to give it a shot."

"Me too," Jeff added, positioning his hand with part of it laying on hers as well as touching Ron's. "I'm adding that I'm giving the three of us a shot, too. I still am not sure what it all means."

Ron pulled his hand out from between hers and Jeff's. "Others go through the same thing. I don't have all the answers either."

Mary glanced at Jeff, easing her hand out from under his. "Thanks for being open to things. I know this isn't easy or what you planned."

Jeff yawned as he stood. "No, it isn't, nor was taking this on tonight. I admit, part of me kept asking if I was nuts. Maybe I am."

Ron rose, turning to her with his arms open. "A good night hug and kiss? I'm going to let you two get to bed."

Mary moved around the table and into Ron's embrace. She whispered as he leaned closer, "I've got condoms. Safe is a priority with me."

"Good. Thanks for sharing." Ron puckered his lips and tilted his head as he tightened his embrace. Mary closed the distance between their lips, her tongue ready to meet Ron's. Instead, he met her lips closed and brushed them lightly over hers. Ron pulled back, winked, and said in a low voice, "Enjoy. I'm restraining myself. You'll get your lullaby soon."

Ron stepped away from her and held his hand out to Jeff. "Treat our lady good, my friend. Welcome home and have a good night."

Jeff didn't offer his hand or take Ron's. Instead, he stepped toe-to-toe with Ron and hugged him, saying, "Thanks. I will. Safe drive home."

Ten minutes passed before Ron stood out in the hallway. He inhaled deeply, stretched his shoulders, and exhaled. He'd done this before and would this time, too. Going home alone when the lady he wanted to spend the night with was spending it with someone else happened in poly. Feelings of being left out sometimes snuck up on him harder than others, like tonight.

He made his way down the hall, not looking back. Dealing with a nagging bit of jealousy didn't help either. Life sometimes threw fast curve balls that hit hard and left marks from its lessons. He was bigger than that. He knew jealousy might be mislabeled envy. As he entered the elevator, one lingering thought tweaked him. What if Mary did choose Jeff over him? His heart skipped a beat and pounded faster as he exited as another fear-jerking thought occurred. What if Mary tossed both of them over? Ron shook his head as he walked out the door toward his car. He looked up as he reached his car. A shooting star shot across the sky. He squinted, focused on his heart's desire, and blew air out his mouth sending his wish out into the universe. Something his mom said one time came to mind—it wasn't what you asked for that counted, it was how you went about getting it that mattered. He got in his car and started down the road home a different person than when he arrived. He'd agreed to a poly relationship. Not something he had in mind when he woke up this morning.

Mary stared at the closed door for several moments.

"Are you okay?" Jeff asked. "Regretting your decision?"

Mary turned to Jeff. "I'm fine. No regrets. Mental what-ifs popping up."

Jeff nodded, yawning again. "Those sneaky pests that make you doubt yourself."

Mary chafed her arms, yawning herself. "Tired thoughts that don't make sense. Let's go to bed."

Jeff held out his hand. She took it and followed him into the large master bedroom.

Chapter Five

Mary smiled as she entered the bedroom. A rumpled blanket and unmade bed greeted her. Looked like she'd be helping Jeff get the place in order like she had when he moved into his apartment. "Sheets and pillowcases? A pillow for me?" she asked, pointing to the bed.

"In the box next to the wall. I'll get you a towel. Back in a moment." Jeff walked out of the room.

Mary shook her head as she tossed the first pillow she came to on the bed, along with a mismatched set of sheets and pillow cases. Organization wasn't one of Jeff's better points. Jeff returned with a large mauve bath sheet draped over one arm. The towel she'd bought for his place. "Thanks for keeping that." She pointed at the towel.

"Got a couple for myself. I love 'em. Let me help you with that." Jeff tossed the towel on the chair close to him. He grabbed the opposite edge of the sheet she tried to shake out.

A few tugs and smooths later, the bed was ready. She walked over to the chair, shucked her clothes, and faced Jeff nude. Her hands at her sides, she gave him the once over and asked, "You gonna stand there gawking or get nude and get in the bed?"

Jeff walked up to her, shucking his clothes, and said, "Your turn to gawk."

Mary gave Jeff a hot once over twice. He'd told her it was her turn to gawk. "Not bad," she said, walking past him. She paused as she got partway past him. She drew her hand back and...

Jeff jumped, yelped, and spun around. "Hey, what do you think you're doing?"

"Getting your attention. Ready for bed?" Mary grinned, grabbed the mauve towel, and walked toward the bathroom. "Is there soap and shampoo in there?"

"Yes, Bev delivered those along with the foodstuff." Jeff followed her.

Mary stopped at the edge of the doorway. "Following me or what?"

"How about a shower together? You know, a quick mutual soap down and rinse off?"

"You don't have ulterior motives?"

"Come on, Mary. I'm too tired to do more than cuddle and snore in your ear. Sorry." Jeff moved past her into the bathroom. "Besides, safe sex practices require condoms. I don't have those."

Mary snorted. "Why don't you get my tote? I came prepared except a sleep shirt."

Jeff gave her a puzzled look, shrugged, and walked out of the bedroom. She entered the bathroom, located the shampoo and soap, along with two washcloths. She closed the commode lid, laid two towels on top of it and walked back into the bedroom as Jeff entered carrying her tote. "I picked up the bag next to your purse off the counter in the kitchen."

"Thanks," Mary said, taking the bag. "In the bag are my toiletry items and a box of condoms."

"You didn't say anything about sex earlier at the shop," Jeff said, looking into the bag and back at her.

"Correct. I decided to be proactive. It's not like I don't find you attractive and didn't enjoy our prior lovemaking."

"And in the tote?" Jeff asked.

"The change of clothes I keep stashed at the shop."

She watched Jeff hold the tote up. "You planned on staying over, didn't you?"

"It was an option. Now it's reality. You asked about a shower?" Mary started toward the bathroom.

"I did. You willing to share one?" Jeff laid the tote on the bed.

"Sure, if there's room for two." Mary stepped into the bathroom carrying the plastic bag. She set it on the dual sink counter and took out the travel-size toiletries, laying them on the counter. Amongst them were two bars of locally made organic soaps.

"Patty's Soaps?" Jeff asked, entering the bathroom. "Didn't know she was back in town."

"She isn't. Her sister is running the business. Patty's overseas with her deployed husband. Japan, I believe." Mary faced Jeff. "I got you a bar of the spearmint musk you like. Peppermint for me."

"Okay. Which one are we going to use? Those two scents don't mix well, remember?"

Mary tittered. "Oh, I do remember that for sure. That was one shower we both agreed we wouldn't forget. You choose."

Jeff picked up the spearmint musk bar. "This beats the over-the-counter one Bev picked up."

Mary pointed to the corner shower stall and grimaced. "That isn't going to hold two of us."

"Correct," Jeff replied, walking across the bathroom. "There's a tub and shower combo behind the sliding door."

Mary watched as Jeff slid the pocket door open, revealing the combo. "I asked for the combo as part of the customization upgrade thinking about babysitting and remembering tubs vs. showers for toddlers."

Mary didn't try to hide her smile. Jeff's thoughtfulness warmed her. Igniting a spark of caring that went deep inside her. This was one reason she'd started dating him three years ago. His concern, caring, and thoughtfulness came through in most of what he said and did. Had even come close to falling in love with him despite their age difference.

"I think we'll fit in here fine." Jeff faced her, holding out his hand. "Care to join me?"

Mary quickly closed the space between them. She took hold of Jeff's hand, kissed his cheek, and said, "I'll wash your back if you wash mine."

"You're on." Jeff kissed the back of her hand and let go. He turned around and bent over, reaching for one of the spigots. His lean, muscular body with six-pack abs and tight pecs hadn't changed. Yes, there were parts of Jeff that hadn't changed, and yet there were. He couldn't be the same, given what he'd gone through. For tonight, she wasn't focusing on that. Tonight was about connection and cuddling. Taking time to reconnect in a way that might permit them a chance to rebuild what they had before. She reached up and wiped away the tear threatening to fall as Jeff stood up.

"You okay?" Jeff asked, turning toward Mary. She shook her head and started to get in the tub. He wasn't going to push limits tonight. They'd already danced along some rough edges and topics. He got in behind Mary and pulled the shower curtain closed. "Water temp okay?"

"Yes. Lukewarm. The way I like it." Mary smiled and reached for the washcloth he offered her. "Thanks for remembering."

"Ten months isn't a lifetime. It feels like it due to the distance that separated us." He reached around Mary and turned the shower on.

Water sluiced over both of them. He stuck his washcloth-covered hand around her and let the water soak it. "I'm washing your back first."

He worked the soap across the cloth until lather appeared. He touched Mary. "Here's the soap. You still like a good back rub as part of washing your back?"

"Sure," Mary answered, taking the soap from him.

Jeff started with Mary's shoulder closest to him and worked the soapy cloth back and forth across her shoulders and back. He stopped close to her ass. Mary thanked him and turned. Her breasts and stomach glistened with soap. His gaze roved lower. Her soap-covered mons greeted him. He licked his lips, wondering if she tasted as good as he remembered, her sweetness coating his tongue as he brought her to orgasm, one after another. Maybe in the morning, he'd find out.

"I remember a bud in here that likes fingertip rubs," he said, rubbing his hand down Mary's soapy stomach. "I'd like to find out."

"Please do," Mary responded, shifting her stance to allow him easy access. "I need and want to come. I was hoping for a quickie."

Jeff chuckled as he combed his fingers through her mons hair. "Quick is key. I don't think I could do more than get semi-erect right now. Hormones are willing. Body's going no fucking way."

Mary rocked toward him as he slipped two fingers between her labia lips. He stroked down and up just short of her clit. He applied two more short teasing strokes. A wet plop sounded. He looked down. A soapy washcloth lay on the bottom of the tub. Mary placed both hands on his shoulders.

He circled clockwise around her clit, grazing the outer edge of it. Two soft gasps told him he hit the right spot. He changed to counterclockwise on his next pass, covering more of her clit, and continued alternating until he covered her clit with both fingers. He quickened his strokes short and fast as he leaned closer to her and whispered, "Come for me. Let me hear and see your pleasure."

Mary tightened her grip on his shoulders, tossed her head back, and rocked her hips back and forth. "Oh My God," she cried out. "I'm going to come."

He sped up his strokes as she moaned and rocked. Her clit pulsed twice beneath his fingers, and wetness coated them. He slowed his strokes and applied lighter touches as she slowed her rocking. Her eyes opened. "Wow. I didn't realize how bad I needed that."

"Glad I could help out," Jeff said. He leaned against Mary, brushing his lips over hers.

"What about you?" she asked, then yawned.

Jeff kissed Mary again. "Wash my back, then see about returning the favor."

"Let me rinse off." Mary ducked under the shower, spraying him at the same time.

He backed up and leaned down retrieving one of the washcloths. He held it up, saying, "Here's the one for my back. I'll use the other on my front."

Mary took the cloth from him. Jeff arched his shoulders as he stood up. Long day cramped in a cross-country flight after an overseas flight didn't help. The antihistamine he'd taken earlier was kicking its second burst in. How much longer he could stay awake, he couldn't say. Their shower play might be what both of them needed to drop into sleep. Mary's touch stroking him to orgasm would definitely put him there.

Mary resoaped the partly rinsed cloth she accepted from Jeff. She handed him the soap and waited while he got his cloth soapy again. "Turn around so I can get your back for you."

Jeff nodded, placing the soap in the soap dish. "You got it." He presented his back and added, "Rub as hard as you can across and between my shoulders. Sleeping sitting up in planes is not easy."

"Poor baby," Mary said and kissed his neck. "Let's see if I remember the spots."

She rubbed and pushed the lathered cloth across Jeff's back, feeling for tight muscles as she did. Those she came across, she rubbed and knuckled like she remembered he enjoyed.

"Thanks," Jeff said, glancing over his shoulder. "That helps a lot. Let me finish soaping the front, and we'll change places."

"You bet." Mary resisted getting out of the shower and back in at the other end of the tub. That took the fun out of trying to work their wet and soapy bodies past each other. Several moments and laughs later, Jeff stood under the shower spray.

Mary held her hand out. "Give me the cloth."

Jeff handed it to her. She worked the remaining lather onto her hand and reached for him. His cock was hard. Not semi-erect like he talked about earlier. She looked up. He smiled and shrugged.

"I think someone fibbed a bit," she chastised, taking hold of him. She stroked upward, loosely gripping him.

"Oh, might have some," Jeff teased. "Not a lot," he added in between groans.

"Well, do I make you wait or take pity and do this?" She stroked up and down, tightening her grasp on each stroke.

"Keep that up," Jeff said in between moans. "And I'm gonna come."

Mary stroked up, stopping short of the head of Jeff's cock. She squeezed and cupped his balls with her other hand. His balls were tight against him. He thrust back and forth through her fingers. She knew that rhythm and pulse. He was ready to come.

Mary tightened her grip, stroked upward and back down fast several times. She looked up. Jeff's head was back. His neck arched with his mouth open. His hands fisted. He cried out on her next downward stroke.

"I'm coming." Jeff shook his head back and forth a few more times and groaned deeply as he stopped shaking.

Mary smiled as she looked at her hand. Streams of white jisim coated her fingers. She leaned forward, scanning her stomach. Lines of male ejaculate coated her. She rose on her tiptoes, kissed Jeff's cheek, and said, "Haven't lost my touch. Glad you had a good come."

Jeff smiled, nodded, and turned around, ducking under the shower. He rinsed off and glanced back at her. "Know you wrung me out good. I'm getting out on this end. Rinse off, and I'll have your towel ready for you."

Jeff stepped out of the shower, splashing bits of water outside the curtain and tub as he did. "Be careful," Mary called out, stepping under the shower and rinsing off.

"I am," Jeff answered. "I put a bath rug in front of the tub to soak the water up."

"Did you forget that before we got in?" Mary asked in a teasing tone.

"Yes, I did," Jeff retorted. "You nude in front of me makes me forget a lot except you."

"Sorry," Mary apologized, turning the shower off and pulling the curtain back. "I had no idea."

Jeff held her towel out to her. He wore his wrapped around his waist. "Don't sweat it. You've got no idea how much you turn me on. It's one of the things we never discussed."

Mary took the towel and wrapped it around her like a sarong. "No, we didn't. I think this is something we need to talk about when we're more awake."

Jeff smiled and patted her cheek. "Much more deep talk, and I'm liable to snore in your ear literally."

"I agree, no more talk. I'm going to brush my teeth and crawl into bed. You got a shirt I can sleep in?"

Jeff followed her to the dual sinks. "One of my t-shirts is best I can do."

"That is fine." Mary moved to the sink near her. She unwrapped her toothbrush and put toothpaste on it. She wet the brush and paste, raised it to her mouth, and hesitated. She looked in the mirror.

Jeff stood behind her, taking in her every move. "What's up?" she asked.

"Remembering the last time we did this." Jeff started to unwind his towel. "Wondering what could have changed the outcome. Made things different."

Mary nodded. "Don't know much could have. Your dad contacted you and said he was dying in a brief call. Susan and Tim moved right after that. We both focused on immediate issues."

"We'd hit a rough patch, too." Jeff hung his towel up. "Each of us wanted more but couldn't meet in the middle."

She shrugged and started brushing her teeth. Jeff had wanted commitment and coupledom. She had wanted a loose connection. He asked to see her more, spend more time together, and that was it. No schedule. No agreement on how often or a public declaration of their relationship. In the middle of this, Darcey had moved back to town. Recently divorced with a precocious three-year-old, Darcey had nowhere to go but home with her.

Mary rinsed her mouth. She caught Jeff returning to the bathroom in the mirror.

He held up a t-shirt. "Do the trick?"

"Yes, thank you." She took the shirt from Jeff and pulled it on. "I stopped sleeping nude."

"Why?" Jeff asked, getting ready to brush his teeth.

"It felt lonely and cold. No one to cuddle with or anticipate the joy of—sex with." She turned away. Damn, she almost said lovemaking. She'd damn near fallen head over heels in love with Jeff. He'd claimed a chunk of her heart and never knew it. She hadn't told him either.

"I'm sorry," Jeff offered. He saluted her with his toothbrush and quickly brushed his teeth. "Maybe we can remedy that some."

"We'll see. I'm crawling in bed." Mary exited the bathroom. Jeff was right behind her.

He got in on the other side, leaned over, kissed her cheek, and said, "Thanks for being here. Sleep spooned and cuddled or apart?"

Mary pressed her lips together. Take a chance on more touch and what? She glanced at Jeff, who held out his hand and said, "Sleep is the only thing on my mind."

She scooted closer, brushed her lips over Jeff's, and turned on her side. He spooned to her, his arm over her waist, and soon his soft snores sounded. Mary moved enough to reach her cell phone. She smiled as she muted the ringer. Ron's home safe text popped up. A simple message they agreed to at the end of an evening. She laid her phone on the bedside table and turned the lamp off. She cuddled back to Jeff, slowing her breathing and feeling content for the first time in quite a while.

Chapter Six

Ron tossed his keys and wallet on his dresser. He yawned as he dropped onto the bed. Three hours later than he anticipated arriving home. His grandmother slept in the guest room down the hall. With his sister, Abebi, and Tabitha down with the flu, he got the job of helping his grandmother, Nana Rose, and four of her girlfriends finish their move to Sacramento. Driving them and the rest of their belongings to the senior housing duplex they'd bought wasn't his idea of a couple fun-filled days. What the movers couldn't fit on their trucks fit in the trailer and Abebi's minivan parked in his driveway. Another yawn overcame him.

He stood and walked to the hamper next to the dresser. He untied his shoes, toed them off, and stripped. He'd pack in the morning. Right now, all he wanted was a hot shower and a minimum of six hours uninterrupted sleep. He reached for the light switch as he entered the bathroom. Bright lights came on. He quickly turned the dimmer switch, dulling the lights to a soft glow. He pulled his towel off the warming rack, draped it over the edge of the soaker tub, and stepped into the glass-enclosed shower next to it. He adjusted the water temperature, turned it on to pulsating, and faced away from the shower. The pounding water spray splashed off his shoulders and down his back.

Ron stretched his shoulders after a few moments, lifted his arms, and reached toward the ceiling. He tipped back until the spray wet his head and hair. After two long slow inhales and exhales, he lowered his arms, tilting his head forward until his neck muscles loosened. He moved his head back and forth along with shrugging his shoulders up and down. Lord, it felt good to stretch and let the pulsing water work the kinks out of him. Running the diner took more out of him than he realized at times. Business grew with the addition of dinner hours, and as the city grew, the catering side increased, too. It was time to hire more help. With Jeff back, would he want back in? Be involved with the business?

Ron picked up his washcloth, squirted shower gel onto it, and worked up a lather. He worked the washcloth over his chest, arms and upper back. He rinsed and bent, easing the sponge and his free hand up and down the front and back of his calves and legs. A quick swipe across his lower back and buttocks left only his cock and balls to wash. He clenched the washcloth in both hands, tightening and squeezing as he worked the lather out of it onto his hands.

He'd fought the dominant images he thought about since leaving Mary and Jeff. If the evening had turned out differently, he wouldn't be dealing with a hard-on that demanded he do something about it. He laid the washcloth on the shelf close to him. He cupped his balls with one hand and started stroking his cock with his other. He closed his eyes, conjuring up his fave image and fantasy of him and Mary. He tightened his hand around him on his upward stroke. He swallowed hard and let out a groan.

Ron caught his bottom lip between his teeth. His balls tightened against him. He fondled them more as he stroked faster. One last stroke upward and—"Yes," he hissed through clenched teeth. The first shot of come started deep down in his balls, blasting its way upward until another tsunami-sized jolt rippled through him, pulling his balls very tight to him, sending two shots of jisim shooting out of him. He let go of his balls as another spurt of jisim dribbled out. He inhaled slowly.

Opening his eyes, he exhaled and reached for the slightly soapy washcloth. He washed off his hands, cock, and balls, rinsed the washcloth and splashed water on the exterior shower wall. He hung the washcloth on its hook to dry as he turned the shower off. He dried off, hung his towel on the rack, and clicked the lights off.

A quick check of his alarm clock showed he had six and half hours until he needed to wake up, get Nana Rose up and ready to pick up her gal pals, as she called them, from the local hotel. She promised him lunch at his favorite Sacramento restaurant in return for making her fave meal of his, Quick Crepes a la Ron. A combination of a thin pancake stuffed with scrambled eggs, diced ham, and monterrey jack cheese. And a pot of Crème Brûlée coffee.

He yawned as he pulled back the covers and lay down on his side. Pillows fluffed and the bedside lamp turned off, Ron closed his eyes, slowly counting his breaths in and out until sleep and post-orgasmic blissed claimed him. His last thought as sleep took full hold was he hoped he didn't snore.

TEN HOURS LATER

Mary rolled over, blinked, and reached for her cell phone. She gripped the phone harder. Nine-thirty a.m. Two text messages showed and a missed call. She glanced over her shoulder. Jeff faced away from her, still sleeping. He rustled, turned over, and reached for her.

"You're too far away. Need cuddles," he said sleepily. His eyes remained closed.

Mary smiled and touched Jeff's hand. "Sorry. It's late and I need to get home. How about I meet you for lunch later?"

Jeff squinted at her, sighed, and nodded. "Sure. I'm sleepy. Gotta get used to this time change." He started to push the covers off.

"Stay put. You've been back a day. Rest and call me when you're up." Mary turned, leaned over and kissed Jeff's cheek. She gathered her clothes and dressed in the bathroom. As she collected her other belongings, Jeff started snoring. Good, he was getting the rest he needed. They could talk later.

Out in the living room, Mary paused, letting the sunlight pouring in through the open blinds soak in. She chafed her arms, shook her head, and pushed her anxious thoughts out of her mind. Things would work out or they wouldn't. Overthinking didn't help. She padded into the kitchen, filled a glass half-full of water and sat down at the table. She reached into her pants pocket and pulled out her phone.

The two texts were from Ron. The first was time-stamped around midnight. His sister and Tabitha had the flu. His Nana Rose was at his place. He was going to bed. The second text was a quick message stating he was taking Nana Rose to Sacramento. He'd call and explain en route.

Mary shook her head as she dialed her voicemail. Ron's nana could be a handful. She'd met the woman and her cohorts a couple of times. They drove hard bargains over the monthly floral contracts for their churches and the senior community center. They were amongst the group that took over the after-school program Susan and Nina started. The five sixty-plus-year-old women kept up with a handful of pre-school toddlers, ten kindergarteners, and a group of fifteen pre-teens who frequented the program. Mary hoped Ron had gotten some decent sleep before taking to the road with Nana Rose and her rowdy gal pals.

She smiled as Ron quickly spoke in his message. The women had filled Abebi's minivan with the last of their boxes and belongings that hadn't made it on the moving vans. They'd managed to fill a moving trailer with stuff, too. He got the job of driving five noisy women, three yowling cats, and four yapping dogs to Sacramento. He asked if she found his sanity cowering on her doorstep to keep it safe until he got back.

Mary burst out laughing as the last of the message played. Nana Rose called out, "Hi, Mary. Don't expect Ron back for a couple of days."

Mary reached inside her purse and took out her spare pill bottle, carefully emptying it into her hand. She swallowed the multivitamin, a fiber supplement tablet, and a birth control pill with the last of the water in her glass. Her gynecologist was right; regulating her irregular periods since she turned forty-five last year made sense. She didn't need another unwanted pregnancy.

She placed her glass in the sink, pulled a sheet of paper off the tablet lying on the counter, and hastily scribbled Jeff a note reminding him to call her later and thanking him for giving her one of his spare keys.

She laid the note on the table, picked up her purse and tote, and entered the living room. She sat on the couch long enough to put on her sandals. She rose, checked the room for any last items of hers, her bags already in hand. As she reached the door, an image flashed through her mind—her lying on a bed between Ron and Jeff. Where was her mind going with this? What had last night's threesome discussion ignited?

Ron glanced in the rearview mirror and prayed. Nana Rose hadn't stopped pelting him with questions about Mary for the last two hours. In between yowls and barks from the four-legged passengers in the back half of the minivan, her friends took turns dispensing relationship advice and asking their own nosy questions. Another forty-five minutes and they'd stop for a late lunch close to the hotel where he'd booked a room. Why had he promised his sister he'd stay until the weekend? Thursday and Friday were his busiest days. And there was the graduation party he had to set up for Saturday afternoon. Good thing he'd planned ahead on that one. Most of the buffet items were prepped. A local bakery was supplying the desserts. Cooking, delivery and set up along with break down were all that remained. He had keys to the country club's kitchen. One of the chefs and several servers would meet him there.

"Ron," Sophia, Nana's oldest friend, said, "Why are you quiet?"

"Sophia," Nana blurted out, "Leave the boy be."

"Boy?" Chella called out from the second-row seat. "I bet he's got a..."

The rest of what Chella said got muffled thanks to Teresa putting her hand over Chella's mouth.

"Couth, ladies. Couth," Faye chastised. "Sorry, Ron. Your love life is your business, not ours."

Ron rolled his eyes and looked at the GPS. A half-mile more and he'd get a break. A simple four-hour drive turned into six thanks to an accident and daytime road work zones. He loved Nana Rose and normally didn't mind chauffeuring her and the gal posse about. This trip they'd overstepped a few boundaries. They'd all watched him grow up. He played with their grandchildren and even babysat a few of the youngest. All five women claimed him as a grandson. How did he tell them nicely that he wasn't discussing his love life or Mary? He cleared his throat, wet his lips, and opened his mouth to speak.

"Ron," Nana Rose said, laying her hand on his arm, "I'm sorry we got out of line."

"Apology accepted, Nana." Ron exited the highway. "Ladies," he continued, looking in the rearview mirror to see the four riding in the second and third-row seats. "I appreciate your concern and advice. No more questions or suggestions, okay? You don't want me asking you about your love life."

Nana Rose chuckled. "Ladies, he's right. Though we did tucker Mr. Anderson out last Saturday night."

"Nana, TMI," Ron scolded, stopping for a light. "TMI."

"Oh, lord, Ron," Nana Rose countered. "The man asked all of us to the community center's dance. He and his poker friends danced with us until midnight."

"Yes, right," Sophia and the rest added.

Ron smiled, leaned over, kissed Nana Rose on the cheek, and said, "Remember I'm too far away to bail you out of jail anymore."

Nana Rose shook a finger at him, grinning. "Maybe we know a bail bondsman or two up here."

The banter continued for the next ten minutes until he pulled into the hotel parking lot. He unfastened his seat belt and turned to Nana Rose. "I think you can all behave until I get back. I'm checking into my room. Then delivering you to the duplex."

"Right. Our move-in assistant, Zoey, is already there ready to let the movers in." Nana Rose winked at him and stuck out her tongue.

Ron laughed, patted Nana's arm, and got out of the minivan. He was going to miss Nana and her friends' banter. They were all family to him as much as his parents and sister were.

The rush of cold air in the hotel lobby wafted over him, sending temporary chills rushing over his exposed arms. July was a few days away, and a Santa Ana wind-induced heat wave was in full swing. Dust and grit were bad enough. Temperatures close to one hundred for several days made him think twice about moving away from the cool breezes living close to the bay offered.

"May I help you, sir?" the desk person asked.

"Checking in," Ron replied, taking his wallet out of his jeans back pocket. "Reservation for Bailey."

"I have you here, sir. Two nights king-size bed non-smoking. Would you like to upgrade to a suite?"

"Not necessary. I saw a couple of restaurants close by. One open twenty-four seven." Ron handed the desk clerk his credit card.

"Yes, they offer senior discounts. A new housing development went in about twenty minutes from here." The clerk handed him his card and his room key.

"Good to know. My grandmother and friends are moving in there." Ron put his card away and put his wallet back in his pants pocket.

"Let them know we offer seniors part-time work. We find they're wonderful workers for our pet sitting or childcare services." The clerk laid a brochure on the counter. "This gives info about it."

Ron picked up the brochure and room key. "Thanks. I'll let them know."

"Enjoy your stay, sir."

"Thank you," Ron said and walked out to the minivan.

As he opened the door, Faye said, "Full house. Aces over deuces. You get to walk the dogs, Chella."

Ron got in, fastened his seatbelt, and said, "Ladies, we're twenty minutes from your new home. Let's get you there and unloaded."

Five yeses echoed through the minivan. As much as he loved Nana and her posse, almost seven hours with them had him ready to comb his hands through his hair several times.

Chapter Seven

Three Days Later

Mary stacked her and Jeff's empty dinner plates as she spoke. "Thanks for stepping in for Ron at the graduation party today."

"Least I could do." Jeff rose, picking up the rest of their dishes off the table. "He helped me out a lot while I was in Europe."

"He's good people. Helped me out, too." Mary entered the kitchen with Jeff following her.

"We gonna talk about Ron or us?" Jeff asked, setting the dishes on the counter.

Mary put the plates in the sink and started rinsing them. Ron's call asking for help took priority. Nursing Nana Rose since she'd come down with the flu kept him in Sacramento. Mary glanced at Jeff and said, "Talk about us. It's been hit and miss with opportunities to do so."

Jeff nodded, opening the dishwasher and taking the plates from her. "Agreed. My question is, what about you and me?"

"I'm not sure we can recapture what we had before." Mary rinsed the rest of the dishes, handed them to Jeff, and shut off the water.

"Okay," Jeff said, putting the last items in the dishwasher and closing it. "Are you saying—there's no us?"

Mary washed and dried her hands. "Not that at all. We can move forward with building a new us or spend time looking backward."

Jeff nodded again. "Where do we start?"

She'd been wondering the same thing. What constituted a good foundation? What supported a relationship? She wet her lips and spoke. "I'm not sure. How about what we have in common?"

"Ona talked about how she and Dad had a contracted marriage agreement their first few years together." Jeff opened the cabinet near him and took out two dessert bowls.

"Sounds complicated," Mary said, placing two spoons and a serving spoon next to the bowls.

"She showed me one of their last contracts compared to an early one." Jeff opened the fridge and took out the container of peach cobbler he'd brought with him. "First one was four pages long and single-spaced. Very detailed. Last one was two single-spaced paragraphs about what they as a couple and family expected from each other."

"Wow. Why did she discuss this with you?"

"Trying to help me understand how and why Dad changed." Jeff set the cobbler on the counter and faced her. "Let's finish talking about this over dessert."

"Ooh," Mary sighed, looking at the cobbler. "Did you bring whipped cream, too?"

"As always," Jeff answered. "Nothing is too good for our sweet teeth."

Mary laughed. "Yes, we sure do have them. Do you want coffee or tea with dessert?"

"Got any of that decaf tea you turned me on to before I left?"

"Sure do. Green container next to the one marked sugar cubes." Mary filled the coffeemaker with water and placed its glass pot on the unit's warming tray. She put two mugs on the serving tray she'd set on the counter. "Going to take ten minutes for the water to heat."

"Okay, I'll put the tea bags and sugar cubes in the mugs." Jeff took two tea bags out and put them in the mugs. As he closed the container, he faced her. "Three sugar cubes still?"

"Yes, please." Mary added the pitcher of cream she got from the fridge to the tray. "I see you got the good whipped cream."

"Once a foodie, always a foodie," Jeff replied, arching an eyebrow and grinning. "I'll get it when we're ready to sit down."

"Let's have dessert and tea in here." Mary sat down at the two-person kitchen table. "How did the graduation party go?"

"It was all right. Every party is unique in some way," Jeff said.

Mary held up her hand, trying to not burst out laughing as Jeff talked about the eighteen-year-old male the party was for. His parents made a huge deal out of his acceptance at several east coast Ivy League colleges. Other relatives toasted him, and several generations of grandmothers, aunts, and other female relatives kissed him so much he had lipstick smeared across both cheeks.

"Oh lord. Poor guy," Mary managed to get out in between snickers.

"By the time his friends came to get him at the end of the party, I think he had a permanent blush going."

Mary quickly covered her mouth. Mirth threatened to spew forth. If the picture her mind came up with matched anywhere near what the teen looked like, he was ready to run out the nearest exit and not come back for quite a while. She took a couple of breaths as she wiped the laughter-induced tears from her eyes. "Sounds like graduation parties haven't changed much."

"Some changes from mine. We pranked a lot. Parents got pissed." Jeff stood, walked to the fridge, and got the can of whipped cream. "What about yours?"

"Did our share of mischief, too. Not like some I've read about or got told about by Darcey and her friends."

"Who's Darcey?" Jeff asked.

Mary took the whipped cream can from Jeff, setting it on the kitchen table. "My step-daughter. She and my granddaughter will be home soon."

"I know you were married before. I don't remember you talking about kids." Jeff sliced into the cobbler and placed a small helping into the bowls next to him.

"That's true. We hadn't gotten to that point before you left. We fell into the relationship because it worked for us."

Jeff faced her. His eyebrows arched as he gawked at her. "Fell into it?"

"Well, yes. Having lunch together a lot got us talking. I mean, we got to dating cuz of shared interests, right?" Mary put detergent in the dishwasher and turned it on.

"I invited you to dinner and a movie we both wanted to see. That's how I ask women out. It wasn't just drinks or coffee." Jeff carried the bowls to the table. "How did we end up in bed together?"

The coffeemaker hissed and gurgled, drawing her from her thoughts. She rose and walked over to the counter. Her hand shook as she reached for the hot carafe. She took a couple of breaths, steadied her hand, and answered, "We've got chemistry. I wanted you, and you wanted me. The second kiss goodnight led to some good making out."

Jeff walked over to her and brushed his lips against hers. "Yes, and a few other goodnight kisses led to absolutely wonderful nights filled with passion and..."

He glanced down, shook his head, picked up the bowls, and walked over to the table. He set the bowls down, sat down, and finished his statement. "You grabbed a huge chunk of my heart and soul. I—"

Mary raced over to the table and laid her fingers on Jeff's mouth, shaking her head. "No, don't say the L word. It's not right. We're..."

Jeff kissed her fingers and pulled back. "Yes, it is right. We fell in love and don't want to admit it. It smacked me upside the head when my gut clenched watching you and Ron together the other night."

"Are you jealous?" Mary asked, gripping the back of her chair.

"Bit by the green-eyed monster?"

"Yeah, that." Mary stuffed her sweaty palm in the pocket of her running shorts. She swiped her palm over the interior fabric twice. They'd been trying to have this conversation for three days with no luck. Neither of them realized how many parties and weddings would take advantage of the discount coupons she and Ron placed in the local and community newspapers. Calls were coming in from San Francisco, Oakland, and Berkeley. Jeff was right. They needed to talk. Wow, had the topic gotten right to the heart matters quickly.

Jeff shot her a weak smile and shrugged. "I'm gonna own it. Yes, I got jealous. I want the connection you and he have. Then I realized I envied you two."

"How so?" Mary turned her chair catty-cornered.

"You have a connection that goes beyond the surface. You're involved in each other's lives. Something you and I missed." Jeff spun his spoon on the table. "How come we did that?"

Mary pressed her lips together. She and Ron had connected because of business and the overflow into their personal lives. Him asking about reliable sitters, Darcey needing job references, and small things like running to the bank or attending community events together. Jeff hadn't shown an interest in that side of things. When had there been an opportunity to? Their partnership with Susan grew out of a mutual business need for each of them. Maybe there wasn't a jealousy or envy issue happening. It was circumstances. People and places along with those involved changed.

"People involved," Mary finally answered. "Circumstances and places, too."

"I don't get it. Explain." Jeff came up next to her, reaching for the mug closest to her.

She continued speaking as she filled her mug. "Darcey wasn't here. We'd gone into business with Susan. Our focus was on growing the business. We just started dating when the business took off. Cascade Bay redevelopment took off."

"And I went to Europe," Jeff added.

"Yes, that too," Mary agreed. "A lot came and went. Could say we got distracted. More focused on business rather than personal."

"What do we do differently this time?" Jeff took his mug to the table. She set her mug on the tray and carried it to the table.

"Talk, connect, and focus on us. I mean, the three of us, too." Mary sat down. She added cream to her tea and stirred. "Balance is going to be a major item."

Jeff set his mug down and pulled his bowl of cobbler to him. "Okay. Balance for me is learning about more of your past. Talk to me about your marriage."

Mary ate two bites of cobbler, laid her spoon down, and wiped her mouth. "What do you want to know?"

"I want to know about your husband. Was your marriage good? His name?"

"Warren and I married right before my twenty-first birthday. Our marriage had its share of ups and downs." Mary drank part of her tea.

"In what way?" Jeff asked in between bites and sips.

Mary pushed her half-eaten dessert away, laid her hands palms down on the table, and waited until Jeff's gaze met hers before saying more. She counted to two and said, "I don't share much of my past with people. I'm not ashamed of who I am. I don't want pity or 'why didn't you' questions. Hear me out first, okay?"

Jeff laid his hand on hers. "Okay. I promise to listen."

"Thanks," Mary responded, sliding her hand out from under Jeff's. She drank more of her tea and faced Jeff. "Warren saved me from a life on the streets."

Jeff's eyes widened, his brows arched. He started to reach for her hand again. She pulled away. "Hold on. Let me finish."

Jeff nodded, pulling his hand back.

"I grew up in Seattle in a middle-income neighborhood. My parents and four brothers adored me. Not a bad thing, you'd think. Except my family believed they knew what was best for me." Mary finished her tea. She stood and walked to the sink, carrying her mug, bowl, and spoon.

"Ouch?" Jeff offered, bringing his dishes to the sink.

Mary laughed. "That would be the lightest description of what I felt. I decided on my nineteenth birthday I had enough and left home with a backpack full of clothes, driving a beat-up car with a half tank of gas and a couple hundred bucks in my purse. Not great preparation."

"Sounds like me deciding to go to college in San Diego and majoring in biochemistry because I got A's in it in high school." Jeff snickered, cleared his throat, and continued, "Only chemistry I got was cooking thanks to my job as a short-order cook to support my living expenses."

Mary patted his shoulder. "Sounds like we both thought we could take on the world at nineteen and twenty."

"Oh yeah. I'll just add, Mom didn't tell me until I flunked out my sophomore year that she and Dad had split up again. This time she filed for divorce. Along with the bank foreclosing on the house, she'd taken a second mortgage out to pay for my attempt at college." Jeff put Mary's uneaten portion of cobbler in the refrigerator. "Go on with what you were saying."

"Damn, Jeff, I didn't know this about you and your mom." Mary tried to hug him. He stepped away.

"I interrupted you. Please, go ahead. When we're done with this part of talking, we can hug and cuddle. Sound good?" He walked back to the sink and rinsed off their dishes. "How about we sit in the living room?"

Mary led the way into the living room, curling up on one end of the couch. Jeff dropped into the recliner close by. He clasped the lever and pushed back. The foot portion came up. He grinned, sighed, and glanced at Mary. "Full stomach, prone, and ready to hear the rest of your tale."

Mary glared at him, shook her head, and said, "You and that chair. Always a fave of yours. Warren, too."

Jeff tried to sit up and grab the lever. "Wh-who's chair?"

Mary laughed and pointed at him. "Warren had an old beat-up recliner. I replaced it with that one. Only you and I've sat in it."

Jeff let go a deep sigh, clasped the lever and sat upright. "I think I can listen better this way."

Mary snorted. "I bounced around Los Angeles for a year and a half going from job to job. Friend's apartment to friend's apartment. A roommate and I decided to move to San Francisco. Worked fine until we both lost our jobs and she decided to get married."

"Left you high and dry?"

"Owing a bill for a motel room and no cash to pay for it. Also second month I missed my period after a one-night stand. Pregnant and homeless."

Jeff grimaced. "You couldn't find the father?"

"Didn't want to. Guy had a low-end job and lived paycheck to paycheck. He owed back child support for the kids from his marriage." Mary sat up, resting her hands on her knees.

"Damn. I'd punch the guy out. That is not right."

"I agree. Reason why I decided to raise the child on my own if I could. Things started looking up. I got a job at a café waiting tables and paid for the motel bill from each check. Warren frequented the café for lunch, and we struck up a friendship."

"Warren sounds like an all right dude." Jeff motioned for Mary to continue speaking.

"He was kind and generous. He put me on to a job at the social services agency he worked for. I was certain I was three and a half months pregnant and needed health insurance. Except that wasn't going to happen. I took a fall walking home from work and miscarried." Mary sniffled and knuckled a tear away.

"Oh, babe," Jeff said, standing and making his way to the couch. He sat beside Mary, slipping his arms around her and hugging her tight to him. "It's okay. You don't have to say more."

"No, I need to get it out. You have a right to know."

He loosened his hold on Mary as she took several deep breaths. "How long were you in the hospital?"

"A week. Warren proposed while I was in the hospital. At first, I said no. He persisted, and with good reason. I couldn't pay the hospital bill without insurance or a job."

"You've survived a lot. No wonder you're a strong woman." Jeff hugged Mary tightly again and let her go.

"Thanks. Warren and I agreed that we needed each other. He had a daughter who needed a mother, and I needed a family. We got married three days before I turned twenty-one. And the rest, as they say, is history."

"When did Warren pass away?" Jeff grimaced, looking away not sure he'd asked a permitted question. "Sorry if I asked a bad question."

"Jeff, look at me," Mary said, touching his arm.

He looked up.

"Not a bad question." Mary kissed his cheek and answered him. "Five years ago. Car accident."

"Please tell me you didn't have to ID his body." Jeff got up and walked over to the fireplace. He looked at the pictures lining the mantel. The one of the two young women always fascinated him. He'd never asked about it.

"A family friend did and broke the news to me." Mary came up behind him and wrapped her arms around him, hugging him tightly.

Jeff pointed to the picture and turned to face Mary. "Who's in the pic?"

"Darcey and I. We're twelve years apart in age." Mary laid her head on his shoulder and sighed. "Before you ask, Warren was fifteen years older than me."

Jeff shook his head, swallowed hard, and blinked. "And you're eight years older than me. What about Ron?"

"Between you and me. Five years younger than me." Mary leaned back, staring at him. "You having issues with this forty-five-year-old woman taking on two younger men?"

Jeff opened his mouth to answer only to be cut off by the front door swinging open and a toddler rushing in, yelling, "G-maw, we're home."

A woman followed behind the toddler, scolding her. "Lindsay, you don't need to yell."

The auburn-haired woman stopped midway into the living room and added, "Hi, Mom. Like Lindsay said, we're home."

Mary let go of him, walked over to the toddler, scooped her up, and kissed her cheek. "Lindsay Marie you're something else."

"I know," Lindsay replied, squirming. "Want down. Need go potty."

Darcey put her purse on the couch. "I'll take her."

Mary put Lindsay down. "Before you do, let me introduce everyone. Darcey, this is Jeff. Jeff, this is my busy bee Lindsay."

"Pleasure to meet you," Darcey said, reaching for her daughter's hand.

Lindsay looked up at him and said, "Are you the poopyhead that made G-maw cry?"

Darcey picked Lindsay up and started toward the other end of the room. "Sorry. I'll talk to her about this."

Mary glanced at him, her eyes glowing with her merriment. She waited until Darcey was out of the room. "Sorry about that. Lindsay hasn't learned discretion yet."

"Well, this poopyhead probably made you cry some," Jeff said, reaching for Mary's hand.

"A few times, yes," Mary said, entwining her fingers with his. "I think we're on the way to better times."

Jeff tugged Mary to him, sliding his arms around her. "Seal that with a kiss, woman, and I'll consider it a signed deal."

Mary pressed her lips against Jeff's. His tongue met hers as their mating dance began. Jeff pulled her tighter to him. She leaned into him, pressing full body upon him.

"Why you kissing G-maw?" Lindsay called out.

Mary closed her lips and opened her eyes as she arched her shoulders, stepping back from Jeff.

"Lindsay," Darcey chastised. "Leave Jeff and G-maw be."

"But Momma, she kissed him like she and Mr. Ron did."

Jeff winked at her and moved back. He turned to see where Lindsay and Darcey were. "I kissed her because I like her. Okay?"

"Okay." Lindsay nodded vigorously.

"Now I get to kiss you cuz I like you," Jeff said, moving toward Lindsay with his arms wide open. "And I'm gonna hug you, too."

"Gotta catch me," Lindsay squealed and took off running.

Jeff hesitated by Darcey. "I'm good with kids. Ask Mary." He trotted into the hallway, calling out, "Lindsay, come mere."

Her high-pitched giggles followed by "Catch me" echoed back down the hall.

Darcey walked over to Mary. "Mom?"

Mary laughed. "Jeff and I babysat Nina and Leslie's twins. Also, Susan and Tim's triplets."

Darcey snickered. "Oh, Jeff is definitely good with kids then."

Mary nodded. "Heard he did a stint or two taking care of preteens while he was in Europe."

Darcey rolled her eyes and pointed toward the hall. "Lindsay loves hide-and-go-seek. We better go help Jeff out."

Chapter Eight

Mary followed Darcey down the hall toward the back bedroom containing Lindsay's various play sets and numerous toys. Darcey stopped at the edge of the open door, motioning her to come closer.

"Oh Lindsay, where are you?" Jeff called out, peeking behind the bedroom door. He waved to Mary and Darcey as he put a finger to his lips.

Lindsay's shrill giggles sounded from one corner of the room. Jeff pointed toward the partially open closet door, nodding. Mary watched him tip-toe across the room and lean down beside the daybed covered with stuffed animals.

"Ah-ha," Jeff said, lifting up part of the bed sham. "Come out I found you."

Mary covered her mouth lest her laughter give her away. Jeff smiled as he turned toward her and Darcey. He pointed toward the closet slowly making his way toward it. "Gee Lindsay, you hide good. I'm gonna find you."

"No, you not," Lindsay yelled as the closet door swung open, hitting the wall with a loud thud. She started across the room toward the door, halting as Darcey moved into the room.

"I think Mr. Jeff needs some help. I'm corralling you." Darcey started moving counter to Lindsay's mad dash toward the door.

"I'm gonna win, Momma." Lindsay started shuffling her feet like she was getting ready to charge forward.

"Oh no," Mary said, moving into the room. "Looks like Momma and Mr. Jeff need my help, too."

Lindsay squealed, stomped her foot, faced her and Darcey, and yelled, "Who gonna help me?"

"I am," Jeff said, scooping up Lindsay. "See, we win."

He held her tight to him, moving forward. "Let's see if we can get by G-maw and Momma, okay?"

"No, want down," Lindsay said, squirming. "Hungry. Momma!"

"Okay, I'll let you down after you give me a hug and kiss." Jeff turned Lindsay so she faced him, his lips puckered.

Lindsay kissed him quick and looped her arms around his neck. "You fun, Mr. Jeff. Now Momma, please."

Jeff kissed Lindsay's cheek and put her down. "Thank you, Miss Lindsay, for a great game of hide-and-seek. You're an awesome hider."

Darcey squatted down by Lindsay, brushing her hair off her face. "What do you say?"

Lindsay shook her head, moving closer to Darcey. Darcey looked up at him, shrugging.

Jeff squatted down by Lindsay, tapped her shoulder, and asked, "Gee, was I that lousy a player?"

Lindsay turned, grinning. "No. I like you, Mr. Jeff. You fun." She threw her arms around his neck and hugged him again.

"Momma, want Chicken Little." Lindsay tugged Darcey's hand.

Darcey stood, took Lindsay's hand, and left the room.

Jeff rose, walked over to Mary and slid his arm around her waist. "I think Lindsay likes me."

Mary laughed. "Oh yeah. She doesn't play hide-and-seek with everyone. It took Ron a few times to get her to play with him and Tabitha. You're on Lindsay's favorite list."

"I could gloat at Ron not making first-string right away." Jeff arched his eyebrows and wiggled his eyes. He glanced at Mary, adding, "I'm not. You and I know kids take to people differently. It took the twins six months to not cry when Nina and Leslie left them with us."

"True. Susan and Tim's triplets took to us like they were ours from the get-go." Mary patted his ass and added, "Not that I am looking for more kids either."

Jeff stuck out his tongue as he faced Mary. "At one point, I wanted them a lot. Now, I've learned to enjoy what life brings me. Darcey and Lindsay are great additions."

"Thanks. Good to know." Mary closed the space between them, looping her arms around his neck. "Loving me includes Darcey, Lindsay, and others in my life like Ron."

Jeff brushed his lips over Mary's. He rested his forehead on hers. "I'm getting used to that. Are you ready for us to use the L word?"

"Mulling it over. Love is a daring proposition for me at this point." Mary stepped away from him. "I know I'm very happy you're back and part of my life again. I think we need to continue to talk about what we want."

"Agreed. I thought about my expectations when I got back. I laid some unsaid ones on you and me. Not fair." He nodded as he continued. "Sorry. I don't like that done to me. Shouldn't have done it to you."

"Don't sweat it. I'm sure I did the same at some point. It happens."

He walked to the bedroom door. "I've got a question."

"Sure. What is it?" Mary joined him.

"Does Darcey know I'm spending the night?"

"We've discussed overnight guests. Darcey knows you're staying."

"Good. What about Lindsay?" Jeff stepped into the hall.

"A little young to discuss sex with her, don't you think?" Mary teased.

"She won't burst in on us?"

"No, she gets if my door is closed to knock and call out G-maw. If I don't answer, I'm still sleeping."

The hall bathroom door clicked open. Jeff glanced over his shoulder as he said, "Sounds great. I don't want to alarm Darcey or Lindsay."

"We'll handle things as they arise. Nothing is set in stone." Mary moved around him.

"Munchkin, I know you want Chicken Little. He's on vacation right now. How about chicken tenders at home?" Darcey asked, following Lindsay out of the bathroom.

Lindsay stopped part way down the hall, her arms tightly folded and a prominent pout going on. She shook her head back and forth rapidly.

Jeff sighed. He leaned toward Mary, whispering, "Twins and triplets all over again. Got the tenders recipe handy?"

"Bagged version along with quick and easy mashed potatoes. Why?"

"Let's make this a family cooking venture. You and Darcey get the tenders in the oven. I'll get Lindsay involved with making mashed potatoes if you have baking potatoes handy." Jeff glanced at his watch.

"How long will the potatoes take?"

"Cube them and put them in the microwave for about fifteen minutes after boiling them. Then mash them up. I only need three to four medium potatoes."

"You're on. The tenders take about thirty minutes to cook two batches. Lindsay can put away the food when it comes to tenders."

"Let me talk to Lindsay," he said, walking toward the pouting three-year-old.

He squatted down and held out his hand palm up. "I like Chicken Little, too. He's a good friend of mine."

Lindsay shoved her hair off her face and glared at him. "Oh?"

"Yes, he gave G-maw and me the recipe for his dinner. We got the tenders in the freezer and I need your help making the mashed potatoes."

Lindsay marched over to Mary. "No fibs, G-maw."

Mary leaned down. "None, my busy bee. Got a big bag of tenders in the freezer. Mr. Jeff will make homemade mashed potatoes if you'll help him."

Lindsay looked back at Jeff, then at Mary. "Okay. Got gravy?"

Darcey laughed. "Yes, munchkin. I got it last time we were at Chicken Little."

Lindsay skipped back to Jeff and put her hand in his. "I love mashed taters."

Jeff rose, holding on to Lindsay's hand. "Good. We'll make a special batch and call them Lindsay's Taters. Okay?"

"Yeah!" Lindsay yelled. "I love Lindsay's Taters." She moved down the hall, pulling him along with her.

Jeff grinned as he looked back at Mary and Darcey. Within a short amount of time, he'd won over Lindsay. Well, at least garnered her good graces. That might not amount for much with Mary. It appeared to win him points with Darcey. She grinned and nodded as he glanced back before scooping Lindsay up to head to the kitchen. Mary's whimsical smile tugged at him. She'd given him that smile once before. The first night he'd asked her to spend the night with him. Maybe he cemented their renewed foundation more with his actions with Lindsay. He'd done them anyway. The precocious imp reminded him of Leslie and Nina's twins, along with Susan and Tim's triplets. He missed the happy-go-lucky interactions with them. Even Ona had shown him the bright, wondrous side of taking care of kids with his youngest siblings. He'd forgotten about that part of life, tackling his father's demise and estate administer duties. It felt good to laugh and play again.

"Okay, Lindsay's Taters here we come," he said, moving down the hall, carrying Lindsay.

"Mom," Darcey said, turning toward Mary. "You okay?"

Mary nodded, exhaling. "Yes. Been a while since I've seen this side of Jeff. He took his dad's death hard."

"I can so relate." Darcey hugged her tightly. "You sure you're okay?"

"Yeah. Remembering how I felt after your dad died. It sneaks up on me from time to time." Mary hugged Darcey back.

"Dad wouldn't want you to be alone. He encouraged both of us to have friends and our own interests."

"He did. Thanks for reminding me." Mary moved out of Darcey's embrace. "Come on, Jeff and Lindsay are in the kitchen making noise."

Darcey laughed as she made her way down the hall. "Let's hope they're not dirtying every pan."

"For sure," Mary added, following Darcey.

Jeff handed Darcey the last plate to dry. Mary sat at the kitchen table sipping her second mug of chamomile tea sweetened with honey. Dinner prep and eating had taken over two hours that he wasn't aware of passing. Mary's large eat-in kitchen had easily accommodated the four of them moving about as preparations and cooking happened. Even when Lindsay had spilled the milk as she added the cup and half to the potatoes he mashed, Mary hadn't reacted. She cleaned up behind Lindsay, telling her to be careful and watch what she was doing to become a good cook like him.

"Thanks for a great dinner, Jeff. Fun having you help with the prep," Darcey said, hanging the damp towel over the rack near the sink.

"Welcome. I enjoyed Lindsay's help. Toddlers have such an interesting view of how the world works." Jeff dried his hands on a paper towel and tossed it in the wastebasket under the sink.

Darcey glanced at her watch. "Lindsay's TV show is almost over. Tomorrow I've got an early day at the daycare center. I'll say goodnight now."

Darcey hugged him. She leaned down, spoke to Mary quietly, gave her a loose hug, and exited the kitchen.

Jeff pulled the chair out across from Mary and sat down. He waited until she looked up before he spoke. "Care to share to share your thoughts?"

Mary drank from her mug and set it down. "Memories mixed with current thoughts."

"Like?" He covered Mary's hand with his.

"Cooking dinner with Warren and Darcey helping out. Then watching you with Lindsay. Wondering if it's fair to you, my not wanting more kids."

Jeff leaned closer, laying his other hand on Mary's arm. "There was a time when I wanted them. I was too young to understand what being a parent was. Now I'm happy to share Darcey and Lindsay with you, as well as the twins and triplets when they're in town."

"You sure?" Mary asked, entwining her fingers with his.

"Absolutely." He squeezed Mary's hand and withdrew his hand from hers. "Ron's got Tabitha, and I bet there'll be times when the three of us will have her and Lindsay together."

Mary burst out laughing. "When that happens, you best take a few extra vitamins. Those two are more than a handful."

Jeff smirked and stood. "Come on. Let's go say goodnight to Lindsay. I promised to tuck her in, remember?"

"She won't let you forget. She'll streak through the house to find you fresh out of her bath. She's done it to me."

"I bet." Jeff picked up Mary's mug as she stood. "We'll say our goodnights and relax in your room?"

"Sounds wonderful." Mary yawned and stretched. "I call dibs on the shower. Need to wash my hair."

"By all means," Jeff responded, taking Mary's hand. "Let's go find Lindsay before she decides to streak."

Jeff glanced at his watch as he laid it on the nightstand. 9:30 p.m. Getting Lindsay settled had taken two stories—one from him and one from Mary—before she settled down with two of her stuffed animals snuggled around her. Darcey had finished with her shower before they had closed Mary's bedroom door.

Mary was in the shower. He pulled his shirt over his head, tossing it on the bed as he heard the shower shut off. A quick shower before he crawled into bed sounded wonderful. Cuddling nude with Mary afterward might lead to some lovemaking. She'd hinted at it as she undressed. He placed his gym bag on the bed and unzipped one exterior pocket. He pulled out a large plastic bag holding toiletry items and opened it.

"All yours," Mary called out from the bathroom. "Plenty of hot water left."

"Thanks. Be there in a moment." He took out a smaller plastic bag containing condom packs and placed it on the nightstand next to his watch. He kicked off his driving moccasins, shucked his jeans and briefs, and laid them on the bed on top of his shirt. He padded nude to the bathroom, carrying his bag of toiletries.

Mary leaned toward him as he moved in front of her to turn the shower on. Her puckered lips told him what she wanted. He brushed his lips over hers and got in the shower. "Sorry for the rushed peck. I want to get the sweat and grime off me."

Mary continued toweling off. "I get you. I'm going to stretch out on the bed."

She hung her towel up, placed one for Jeff on the counter, and exited the bathroom. Normally she'd put on her nightshirt, crawl in bed, and read for a while. Tonight, she pulled back the covers and got in bed nude. Jeff's clothes and gym bag occupied the opposite side of the bed. He'd take care of putting his stuff away before he got in bed. They'd agreed early in their relationship each picked up behind themselves.

She combed her fingers through her partially dry hair. By morning, her natural curls would stand out, and all she'd need to do was run a brush through them.

"Man, I feel better." Jeff exited the bathroom, grinning. "Thanks for laying the towel out for me."

"You're welcome."

She turned on her side, watching Jeff fold his clothes and put them in his gym bag. He put his bag on the floor, his moccasins on top of it, and faced her.

"What time do you need to be at the shop?" he asked, getting into bed and laying on his back.

"Noon. Carena is opening." Mary scooted closer to Jeff until she could lay her head on his shoulder.

"Good. I've waited to do this until now." He reached under the sheet, cupped her breast, and stroked her areola with his thumb. "Touching you is important."

"Hmmm, that feels good." She turned on her side. Pulling her pillow to her, she tucked it under her head. "I want you."

"I want you, too." Jeff turned on his side and cuddled close to her. He placed a leg over her hip and reached for her breast with his hand. He captured her nipple between his thumb and finger, twisting it as he leaned closer to her.

Mary slipped her hand between them, reaching lower until she brushed Jeff's hard cock. He oozed pre-cum that wet and lubricated her fingers as she ran them over and around his glans. "You're wet," she whispered as Jeff pressed his lips against hers.

Their tongues met. Tasting and touching the other as sips and nuances of each blended with their own essence. The kiss continued for several more moments. Jeff pulled back, groaning. "I need to come."

"I want you to come inside me." She stroked down Jeff's cock until she reached his balls, cupped them, squeezed lightly, and stroked back up, letting go as she reached the end of him.

Chapter Nine

"Yes, sweetness. I love pleasing you," Jeff whispered, sliding his hand down Mary's waist until pubic hair tickled his fingers. Mary rocked toward him, pushing her mons beneath his hand. He slid his hand lower until her wetness, and swollen nether lips grazed his fingers. Slipping two fingers lower, he coated them with her wetness as he reached her clit. Taut, pulsing, and swollen like her nipples, he stroked back and forth, suckling her nipple in contrast to his clitoral caresses.

"Ohhh," Mary gasped, gripping his shoulder. "Multiples."

Jeff stopped suckling, concentrating on fast, short strokes across Mary's clit. "Yes. Let me bliss you out."

He continued stroking until Mary tapped his shoulder. "No more, *please*. My clit is very sensitive."

Jeff picked up Mary's hand, laying it on his cock. "What you going to do about this?"

Mary raised her head and looked down toward where his hand covered hers. "BJ? Give me a moment to catch my breath."

"No BJ tonight. Want to come inside you." He jerked as Mary firmly stroked his cockhead, working her way down to his balls and back up. "Let me get a condom on. Can you roll on your side toward me?"

"Yes," Mary said, rising up on her elbows. "Need help with the condom?"

"No. I'll get it on faster without help." He rolled over, sat up, and pulled a foil packet out of the small plastic bag. Ripping the packet open, he glanced over his shoulder. Mary lay on her side, facing him. She rested her head on one shoulder, watching him.

Jeff looked away, needing to concentrate on getting the condom on in one piece. He eased the condom out of the packet between his thumb and fingers. Palming the condom as best he could, he worked it down and over him until he touched his balls. Taking a deep breath, he scooted back and turned. He laid back, holding his hand out to Mary.

"Come have your way with me."

Mary got up on her hands and knees and started working her way back down the bed until she reached Jeff's waist. Taking hold of Jeff's hand, she steadied herself as she swung one leg over him, straddling his waist. She gently clasped his cock and guided him into her.

"Oh man, you're wet and snug," Jeff groaned, letting go of her hand and lifting his hips off the bed. "Easy on me, okay?"

"Easy?" Mary quipped. "Oh no. I've waited for this. Now I ride."

She rose slowly, contracting around Jeff. Watching Jeff, she sunk back down. Jeff's eyes closed as he bunched the sheet in one hand. His other gripped the pillow his head laid on. Mary smiled and started a slow rocking back and forth motion, contracting on her backward rocks and letting go with each forward one.

"I need to come," Jeff groaned. "On sides, please?"

"Sure," Mary answered, her own need heating up deep within her. She rolled to her side, causing Jeff to slide partway out. She reached between them, taking hold of him as he rolled toward her.

"Easy," Jeff cautioned. "Don't wanna tear the condom. I don't think I could get another on and stay hard."

"Losing interest?" she asked, squeezing him slightly.

"No-oo," Jeff groaned. "Hard too long, and blue balls happen."

"Come closer and slip back inside me then." Mary started closing the gap between them.

"Sorry, babe. I need you to come to me." Jeff slowly rolled onto his right side, pushing his cock up through her encircled fingers. There was no mistaking his reaction. Every breath he took shook his chest. Short breaths, no matter how many he took, told her he wanted her.

Mary moved closer until her leg touched Jeff's. Murmurs of needing a pictorial guide to Kama Sutra positions filled the air. Soft giggles followed. Moments later, sighs of passion bubbled forth. Mary tangled her fingers in Jeff's hair as she pulled his head down to her, and she captured his lips with hers.

Jeff broke off the kiss, gulping air. He raised his left leg, creating enough space for Mary to put her leg over his right until she brushed against him. With her help, he slid back into her warm, wet tightness. She rocked toward him as he rocked back. To and fro, back and forth, until he couldn't tell if he'd thrust in or pulled back. He reached up, combed Mary's hair off her face, and watched her through partially closed eyes. She flushed from her neck up and part way down to the v between her breasts. Her breath came in short gasps the faster she rocked with him. He licked his finger, reached between them, and found her clit. He rubbed in small, tight circles over and around the pulsing bud until Mary called out.

"Oh my god! I'm coming," she cried out and started shuddering.

Mary sucked in air and rocked toward Jeff. His finger swept over and around her clit in tight small circles. Every time she pulled back, he stroked upward as he thrust into her. "Can't take much more. Big one now."

Her eyelids slammed shut, blocking out Jeff. Purples, followed by deep vivid shades of red and orange, exploded across her field of vision. Colors that drew her attention as she arranged flowers and chose decorations. A kaleidoscope of color bursting and exploding one after the other until she couldn't tell where one started and the other finished. Wave after wave of deep, intense pleasure welled up inside of her, pounding through and over her until she tightened around Jeff and held still.

Jeff gripped her shoulder and whispered, "Sorry." He groaned as he thrust deep into her, jerking his hips back and forth.

Mary squinted as the colors decorating her vision began to fade. Jeff came into view. His head was back, arching his neck as he gasped in between moans and groans. He pulled partway out, stopped, and plunged into her, groaning, "My turn to com-m-e-e."

Moments passed. Neither of them moved. Mary took several deep breaths, counting to five with each inhale and exhale, waiting for her heart rate to return to normal. Jeff let go of her shoulder. He lowered his neck and head until she could fully see his face. He looked at her with one eye, smiled, and said, "*Wow*."

"*Wow* indeed." Mary yawned, blinked, and yawned again. "Sleepy."

"Me too." Jeff slowly untangled his legs and arms from hers and laid on his back.

Mary rolled away from Jeff onto her other side and sat up. "I'm going to the bathroom."

"Okay," Jeff sleepily replied. "Gotta remove condom and..." His voice trailed off. Mary smiled as his chest rose and fell, followed by soft snores.

She moved around the bed, took a tissue from the box on the nightstand, gingerly eased the condom off Jeff, and wrapped it in the tissue. Jeff murmured something unintelligible and turned over. Mary shook her head, walked into the bathroom, and discarded the condom in the wastebasket beneath the sink. Five minutes later, her bladder empty, her hands washed twice, she turned off the lamp, pulled the covers over them, and cuddled Jeff. One last thought formed as sleep possessed her. Did she risk her heart again? Risk it twice with two men at the same time?

Buzz! Buzz! Jeff blinked, squinted with one eye and reached out with one hand, ready to hit the snooze button. Except there was no clock, and the buzzing kept getting louder. He blinked again, raising his head off the pillow and glancing at the sunlight dancing across the wall from the partially closed blinds. Yawning, he tried to sit up. The sheet covering him went taut across his chest. He grabbed the end closest to him and tossed the sheet aside.

"Hey," Mary said in a muffled voice. "Watch where you're throwing things!"

He quickly turned over, capturing his bottom lip between his teeth lest he burst out laughing. Mary lay next to him trying to get untangled from the sheet he'd inadvertently tossed over her. "Sorry," he said, pulling part of the sheet toward him. "Forgot where I was as I woke up."

Mary worked the rest of the sheet off her. She shoved her hair off her face and sat up. "Don't know if that's good or bad."

Jeff sat up, tossed the sheet completely off them, and scooted across the bed until he sat next to Mary. "It's real good. Best deep sleep I got since getting back."

Buzz! Buzz! Buzz!

Mary moved to the edge of the bed, picked up her cell phone, and rose. "Damn, has Darcey overslept again? That's the backup text from her carpool partner."

Jeff pulled on his jeans, not bothering with his briefs. He hastily fastened and zipped them. He reached for his moccasins. "You check on Darcey. I'll run out and let the driver know she's running late."

"It's her day to drive." Mary pulled on her robe as she walked toward the door. "I'll check on her. You check on Lindsay, please."

"Got ya." Jeff pulled on his shirt and started down the hall toward Lindsay's room. The door was open. Quiet greeted him as he looked into the room. Lindsay's bed was empty. Had she crawled in with Darcey?

He turned, ready to head across the hall to Darcey's room, when he heard Mary say, "No problem, Nathan. I'm glad Darcey picked you and Jaxson up early. Thanks for letting me know you're all safe. Bye."

Jeff closed the space between him and Mary. He held his hand out to her. "Everything okay?"

She took his hand, nodding. "Yes. A big rig jack-knifed out on Lakeshore Boulevard coming off the interstate. Darcey usually takes that route when she's driving carpool."

"She's okay?" He slid his free arm around Mary's waist, ready to hug her.

"She's fine. I forgot a new guy is carpooling with her and Nathan. She took a different route since Jaxson lives the furthest out."

Jeff hugged Mary and let go. "Good. How you doing?"

"A bit frazzled waking up abruptly. Otherwise, I'm fine." Mary moved away from him. "I need a quick shower after last night."

Jeff chuckled. "I do, too."

"I'll use Darcey's and you use mine. I'll meet you back in the bedroom in ten minutes." Mary entered Darcey's room, calling out, "No time for morning after sex this time. Sorry."

Jeff smirked, shook his head, and entered Mary's bedroom. He quickly stripped off his clothes and moccasins. Mary didn't give time frames unless she meant them. He knew better than to make her wait to meet in the bedroom, dressed or not.

Ten minutes later, he emerged from the bathroom toweling off. He looked around and found Mary looking out the window. He wrapped the towel around his waist, moving around the bed. "Something wrong?"

Mary rubbed her arms, shaking her head as she faced him. "Not really. The accident ignited memories and emotions that pulled me back in time."

"Care to talk about it?" he asked, taking off his towel. He pulled on clean briefs and a t-shirt as he continued talking. "It's never easy when those reach up and coldcock you. Went through that with my dad. 'Nam vet suffering from PTSD."

"How'd you handle that?" Mary took hold of his hand and squeezed it.

"It wasn't easy at times. He would talk and go silent. Sometimes he'd call out in the middle of the night, screaming he needed to talk before it ate him up more." Jeff let go of Mary's hand. He pulled clean jeans out of his gym bag and put them on. He caught hold of Mary's hand as she started to walk away. "Do you need to talk about what you're feeling?"

"Mixed emotions. Sad Warren won't get to meet Lindsay. Happy Darcey is dating again. Her ex hurt her real bad. Wondering about you, me, and Ron." Mary took off her robe and hung it on the back of the bathroom door.

Jeff pulled on a clean polo, folded his dirty clothes and put them in the gym bag. As he put his moccasins on, he spoke. "I understand some. I can't say I get it all."

Mary put on one of the embroidered pastel polos she wore to the shop. She walked to the closet close to him and took out a pair of jeans. "We're not going to solve some of life's problems chatting about them. You gotta live. Life is a great gift."

"For sure," Jeff agreed, picking his towel up as he came around the bed. "We'll work on this together. You, me, and Ron."

Mary smiled, taking the towel from him and tossing it in the hamper. "For now, we need to talk about Lindsay's birthday party in two weeks. One of the texts was from Ron."

"Busy bee Lindsay queen bee for a day," Jeff quipped.

Mary laughed. "Darcey's helped Ron with several parties. He's helping her with this one."

"Ron's working the party planning side of the business?" Jeff walked back around the bed, picked up his belt, and threaded it through his jeans' belt loops.

"Sometimes. We've made connections through customers and clients. It's part of the business we need someone to oversee full time."

"Susan traveled a lot for those. Is that still true?"

"Yes. Darcey's talked about taking the job on full time since she's moved back home." Mary tied her sneakers and stood. "I can take care of Lindsay while she travels."

"More babysitting duties?" Jeff handed her her watch and walked to the bedroom door. "We're going to have our hands full."

"If you mean you, me, and Ron—*oh yeah*. Lindsay and his niece Tabitha are best friends."

Jeff faced her, shaking his head. "Taking care of a rambunctious three-year-old and four-year-old isn't the same as five two-year-olds."

Mary snickered. "True. Lindsay and Tabitha can be a handful if they're arguing. Doesn't happen often, but when they do..." She stopped speaking as Jeff held up his hand.

"Can't scare me off. The three of us will handle it." Jeff turned and walked out the door, adding, "I never expected to get this deeply involved with Ron and everyone's family this quickly."

Mary pressed her lips together, wondering if Ron felt the same way. Sex wasn't part of their relationship yet. They'd hinted at it. Even discussed it before the three of them had talked two weeks ago. Sometimes things happened quickly. Others moved slower. Ron said moving at a speed all felt comfortable with mattered. And there was the poly mantra—communicate, communicate, communicate. Maybe this was the process aspect he said some polys disdained. Did Jeff feel things were moving too quickly?

"Do you think the three of us are moving too fast?" Mary asked, entering the hall.

Chapter Ten

"D on't know. Remember, I'm a poly newbie." Jeff turned as he reached the end of the hall. "I hadn't given things much thought beyond us three."

Mary nodded, taking ahold of Jeff's hand. "Me either. Maybe we can get together with Ron and talk this week."

"Can't. I'm going to Sacramento to interview chefs for Susan's new restaurant."

"Sorry, I forgot." Mary crossed the living room. "You cooking breakfast, or am I?'

"I am. Lets me at least honestly say I'm still cooking and a foodie," Jeff replied, moving past her into the kitchen. He turned, leaned down, and brushed his lips over hers. "All's good. Have fun with Ron while I'm gone."

Mary slipped her arms around Jeff's waist, hugged him tightly, and stepped back. "Thanks. Lindsay's going to miss you, too."

"I'll be back in time for her party. Tell her Mr. Jeff likes to party."

Forty minutes passed while they fixed breakfast and talked about Lindsay's party.

"Be right back," Jeff called out, entering the living room. "I'm going to get the paper."

"Thanks," Mary replied, placing plates loaded with omelets, potatoes, and toast on the table. She added utensils, the sugar bowl, and the cream pitcher. Jeff came back in as she filled their mugs with coffee.

"Smells awesome in here," Jeff said, entering the kitchen carrying the paper. "Crème Brûlée coffee. Haven't had it since my last trip to New Orleans."

Mary separated the paper by sections as she sat down. "I get monthly sample packages from a local supplier. Variety for home and the shop."

Jeff picked up his mug and sipped. "Black and sweet already. And no grounds. Never developed a taste for espresso."

"Too strong. Can be bitter if improperly brewed. And the coffee grounds. No thank you. I still prefer tea overall." Mary handed Jeff a napkin.

"Different tastes all over. Regional and eclectic for sure." Jeff handed her the entertainment section. "Crossword looks to be a doozie."

Mary picked up the pen she'd laid on the table and began working the puzzle as she ate. Jeff folded open the front section and laid it next to his plate, eating as he read.

Mary laid the pen down thirty minutes later, wrapped her hands around her coffee mug and rubbed her lips together.

She watched Jeff fold the morning newspaper in half and lay it on the table. He rose, reaching for her plate. "You done eating?"

"Yes," she replied, laying her hand on Jeff's arm. "There's something I want to ask you."

Jeff turned his chair toward her and sat back down. "Go ahead. You've been quiet since I handed you the crossword puzzle."

"Our discussion on threesomes..." She deliberately paused, knowing what she said next could make or break the discussion moving forward.

Jeff rocked back in his chair, almost tipping it backward. He grabbed the table's edge, righting himself and the chair as he spoke. "Damn, you know how to catch a guy off-guard."

Mary smiled weakly. "Take it easy. I've been thinking about three-way nude cuddles...."

Jeff stared at her for several moments. Shook his head and looked away. He rose, picked up their plates, and walked away. She scooted her chair back, ready to go after him, when he turned back to her. "It takes three. There's only two of us."

Mary walked over to Jeff, took the plates out of his hand and set them in the sink. She looped her arms around Jeff's waist and hugged him tightly to her. "I said I was thinking about it. I wanted to know if it intrigued you."

Jeff turned in her arms until he faced her. He rested his forehead against hers. She could feel every breath he took. He closed his eyes as he answered her. "More than intrigued."

"Oh?" Mary stepped back until she could see Jeff's face clearly.

"I got—got turned on." Jeff put his hands on her shoulders, pushing lightly as he started to move away.

She copied his moves, not away from him, but with him, letting her stay right with him. Every time he stepped back, she moved forward, not letting him create any more space between them. She glanced around Jeff on his next move. He wasn't going much further unless he wanted the backdoor knob permanently inserted somewhere.

"I asked. You answered. Do you hear or see me scolding you?" she asked, cupping Jeff's cheek.

Jeff's gaze met hers. "No. Based on what you said before, I got the idea the topic was off-limits."

"I understand. I agree that is probably how I felt then. Like me catching you off-guard right now." Mary slid her hands off Jeff's shoulders and down his arms until she reached his forearms.

Jeff stepped away from her, moving toward the table where his duffle bag sat on a chair. He picked his keys up off the table, putting them in his jeans pocket. He picked up the utensils and mugs, put them in the sink, and faced her. "You're saying you want a three-way cuddle?"

"I'm curious and want to know more." Mary handed Jeff his duffel bag. Mary opened the back door and walked out onto the deck. She started down the steps when Jeff called out, "Don't forget your purse." He leaned out the door, holding it out to her.

"Thanks. Not leaving yet. I want to put the dishwasher to run before I leave. I also need to make a couple of calls," she said, glancing at her watch.

"I put your purse on the counter," Jeff said, moving past her. "Everything okay?" he asked, continuing down the steps and stopping at the driveway's edge.

Mary looked up. "Yes, I need to check if two special orders are ready for pick up at the flower market."

She made her way down the steps and stood next to Jeff. She took hold of his hand and squeezed it. "Really, we're good. I run errands on my late start days."

"All right. Walk me to my car?" Jeff asked.

"Sure." Mary leaned close and kissed Jeff's cheek. "I care. Please let me know you arrived."

"I'll text you when I get to Sacramento." Jeff slipped his arm around her waist and hugged her. They talked for a few more moments after Jeff got in his car. He reassured her he was good with her spending time with Ron even with him still needing to wrap his head around the three of them.

Mary stood next to her car as Jeff pulled out of the driveway. She agreed with him on a couple things he said. They needed to talk more, as well as Ron and him. Even she and Ron needed to discuss him and her. Maybe Jeff's trip would give her and Ron time to talk.

Mary walked back inside. She picked up her purse and laid it on the table. After loading the dishwasher and turning it on, she opened the drawer close to the back door and took her daily planner out of it. Her cell phone rang as she put the planner on the table and sat down. The caller ID showed Ron's number. She answered on the third ring.

"Hi, studly," she teased in a low, husky voice. "What ya up to?"

Ron's laugh caressed her ear even though their phones and several hundred miles separated them. "Hi, your sexy self. I'm done with nursing the sick. Much more and I'm certain my sanity is fleeing."

Mary put her hand over her mouth trying to contain her laughter. She burst out laughing at Ron's next statement. "As if getting propositioned by the new members of Nana Rose's cadre isn't bad enough—they're trying to set me up with the housing assistant, Zoey."

Mary put the phone on speaker, laying it on the table as she laughed harder. As she caught her breath, she asked, "Ron, what else have you been up to?"

"Learning Nana Rose cheats wickedly at Pinochle and Gin. Never know what you may find out when you nursemaid your grandmother and her gal pals." Ron chuckled as he added, "Zoey said go home before the group stirs up more shenanigans."

"Are you sure it's safe to leave them unchaperoned?" Mary asked, pulling the phone closer to her as she opened her planner.

"Yes. They all had dates for Saturday night's dinner and dance at the community center," Ron replied. His sigh of relief came through the speaker loud and clear. "I'm on my way back. I got an interesting text from Jeff."

"You did?" Mary laid the pen she'd been holding down.

"Yes. Something about nude three-way cuddles."

Mary pressed her lips tightly together, trying to keep her groan silent. How did she respond? How much had Jeff said? A few questions and a short discourse didn't equate yes she wanted one.

"Well...I...hmmm," Mary began, going silent, unsure what to say further. She hadn't given the topic a lot of thought. She still had unanswered questions and unexamined feelings.

"You curious about them?" Ron asked after several moments.

Mary inhaled, wet her lips, and answered. "Curious some."

Ron paused, then added, "Don't damn your curiosity."

"I hear you. It's... I'm not sure how to say this."

"Go ahead. Say what you're feeling," Ron encouraged.

"The videos and pics left me cold. Disconnected and at six-and-sevens."

"I got you. I understand not getting turned on by watching others doing it. I've had cuddles that left me flat. No connection or chemistry happening," Ron said.

"Then why do them?" Mary asked, twirling her pen on the table.

"Because there's good ones, too. Sometimes you don't know who you'll connect with," Ron said, horns sounding in the background. "I'm hitting traffic. How about I meet you at the shop later to discuss this more? Say, over dinner?"

Mary opened her planner and ran her finger down the entries. "I also need to talk with you about an upcoming wedding that needs catering. Dinner sounds wonderful. Meet at Ranagian's around six-thirty? Safe drive."

"Good with me. I'll see you then. Bye." Ron ended the call.

Mary added Ron to the bottom of the entries for the day. She picked up her phone, called the flower market to verify her orders were in and discussed the arrangements they were working on for an upcoming quinceanera party. Two more calls had her scratching off the top five entries. She glanced at her watch and pushed back from the table. Walking out to her car, one thing nagged her. Why had Jeff texted Ron about their discussion?

Mary eased her way into the noontime traffic making its way onto Main Street and toward restaurant row. A horn honked, breaking her train of thought. She pulled into a parking space close to the flower market's entrance.

Forty-five minutes passed before she was on her way to the shop. The back seat held several bundles of flowers. The lilac bunches filled the air with their soothing scent, mixing with the bouquet the dried lavender packets emitted. Her car smelled sweet, fragrant, and soothing. If only taking a few deep breaths would convince her psyche to concentrate on traffic.

Mary knew focusing her thoughts on business and clients wasn't going to be easy. Not where her thoughts were otherwise. She had ten minutes to get to the shop, get Carena on her way to lunch, and meet with the parents planning the quinceanera celebration. Thanks to a lull in traffic and good luck making a left-turn green arrow, she got to the shop in eight minutes. As she pulled into the rear parking lot, she gripped the stirring wheel tighter. Every parking space assigned to the shop was full, except her reserved space. Keeping her mind on work just got easier. How long the rush would last, she didn't know.

SIX HOURS LATER

Mary closed and locked the door as the last client exited the shop. She walked behind the counter and into the short hall leading to the design room and her office. Carena sat at the worktable talking on the phone in Spanish with a client. She nodded and pointed to the pad as Mary got closer. Mary leaned down, looking at the pad. Her mouth dropped open. Orders for two more quinceanera festivities topped the pad. The line below read, 'Three more referrals coming in, plus possibly more.' Mary nodded and patted Carena's shoulder, giving her two thumbs up.

Mary walked into her office, leaving the door open. She waited until Carena finished speaking with her client to call her into the office. "Carena, come on in for a moment, please."

Carena sat down in the chair in front of the desk. "What a busy day."

"Yes. I'm wondering if you're interested in full-time. We've got a growing Spanish-speaking clientele. If you want it, the position is yours."

Carena leaned forward. "I accept. When my prior job shut down, I didn't think I'd find work I enjoyed. I found a better one."

"Have you?" Mary asked, passing Carena a benefits package folder.

"Oh, I have. One that lets me put my creative side to work. Thank you for hiring me full-time. I'm not ready for full-time retirement yet." Carena started to open the folder.

"Take it home and read things over. We'll talk more in the morning." Mary stood. "I'm glad your retirement just became part-time."

Carena left out the back door ten minutes later. Mary shut off the lights and locked up. As she walked to her car, she glanced at her watch. 6:15 p.m. She had fifteen minutes to get across town and meet Ron on time. She hoped traffic had died down some.

Chapter Eleven

R on glanced at the car's dashboard clock as he pulled into Ranagian's parking lot. 6:35 p.m. He spotted Mary waiting near the entrance as he parked. He honked the horn and waved as he got out. Mary waved and started walking over to him. He met her halfway, taking her hand as he leaned in and kissed her cheek. "Sorry I'm late."

"I just got your text. Didn't realize I muted my phone. Glad you made it." Mary brushed her lips over his. "I'm hungry. Shall we go in?"

Ron nodded. "Yes. I'm famished. Drove straight through. Dropped the minivan at Abebi's. Jumped in my car, and here I am."

"I read the specials menu. Pork chops glazed with maple sugar, choice of sides caught my eye when I put us on the waitlist." Mary held the door open.

Ron opened his mouth to speak, instead a loud growl from his stomach sounded. He looked down, back up at Mary, shrugged, and smiled. "I think I've been told what my choice is."

Mary laughed. "I agree."

Inside, the host guided them to a table in the quieter section of the dining area. Their server took their drink and food order. As the server walked away, Mary sighed. "I'm not sure where to start. I can't figure out why Jeff texted you."

"Questions. He's unsure. Wants to support you. And, in a way, us." Ron leaned back against the booth's cushioned back. "Can you say why you brought three-way cuddles up?"

Mary blew air out and answered, "Curiosity. Trying to understand. Goes back to Warren and his buddies asking for a stripper and all the bachelor party stuff. Their explanation about it being a guy thing never made sense."

"Sorry you got nothing concrete to help you then. I can tell you my side only. Can't speak for others." Ron spread his napkin across his lap.

Mary waited until their server placed their drinks and bread on the table before answering. "Thanks for what you can answer. I know some women like watching sex clips. I don't."

Ron tore a piece of bread off the loaf, buttered it, and laid it on the plate next to him. "Have you ever watched a movie or read a book where you got juicy? Kept reading or watching because you connected with what is going on?"

"Yes. Even with some TV series." Mary stirred her ice tea as she added sweetener.

"My piece of bread was part of the loaf. The whole loaf appeals to me," Ron began, holding up his piece of bread. "My enjoyment of it is bite-by-bite. You might savor yours with butter or without. And fold it in half, eating it that way."

Mary pointed a finger at Ron, partly opened her mouth, and closed it. She drank some of her ice tea and rubbed her lips together. She inhaled and swiftly exhaled, nodding as she picked up an empty sugar packet close to Ron's glass of ice tea. "It's like you like sugar in your tea. Where I like sweetener in mine. A matter of taste and what connects. Right?"

"Basically, yes. Matter of personal likes and choices. That's where it starts." Ron bit into his piece of bread and chewed.

Mary laid the sugar packet down. She leaned forward, resting her elbows on the table. "I get that. But with a book or TV show, sex isn't the only thing. There's emotions and other stuff happening."

"Right," Ron said. "That's the crux of why some relationships work and others don't, too."

"Because they're all not on the same page?" Mary dropped one hand into her lap, clenching her napkin with it.

"Communication and connecting isn't happening. When you assume…" Ron paused.

"You make an ass out of you and me," Mary added. "I hope I haven't done that to you."

Ron pushed his bread plate aside and reached around both of their glasses. He touched her forearm as he spoke. "Never. We've had communication faux pas. Nothing that we didn't correct. We're talkers. Doers. Someone like Jeff who is more introverted might be quieter about an oops."

"Meaning he internalizes it?" Mary let go of her napkin and patted Ron's hand.

"Can't say. We're extroverts. Talk things out. Think out loud. Jeff is great with people he knows or when it's a topic he's familiar with. Introverts tend to be silent thinkers and look for deeper intrinsic value."

"I'm a bit of both. Though extrovert is my stronger aspect." Mary nodded as she continued speaking. "Now I get why Jeff texted you. He's keeping us on the same page while expressing his concern."

Ron pulled his cell phone out. "I'll share Jeff's text with you because it concerns the three of us."

"Yes, one poly communication rule I totally agree with. If it is not yours to tell, don't."

"Remember there are exceptions to every rule. What if it affects all three of you like this does? Or may hurt your love?"

Mary picked up the remaining piece of bread and held it up. "Concealing isn't good. Neither is lying. Trust is very important. Like this bread heel is part of the loaf's foundation, so is being truthful and upfront with each other."

"Yes. Sometimes you have to nudge the two parties together who need to talk. Isn't always easy. But it often yields stronger and better relations between everyone." Ron held up his hand. "Here comes our dinner."

The server set two plates with maple-glazed pork chops, loaded baked potatoes, and steamed broccoli buds on the table. "Anything else?"

"More bread." Ron handed the server the empty bread plate.

"And more butter for the broccoli." Mary set the empty butter bowl on top of the bread plate the server held.

"Very good. I'll be back with the bread and butter shortly."

Mary waited until the server was several tables away before she spoke. "Thanks for sharing Jeff's text. What does it say?"

Ron held his phone up, leaned forward, and said, "Mary's curious. Three-way nude cuddles. I'm not sure. Your take, please."

Mary picked up her knife and fork, cut into one of her pork chops, and speared the piece of meat. "Sounds to me like this is a puzzle needing all the pieces to come together. We're each one."

"I agree," Ron said, cutting into his pork chops. He held up his fork, reached over, and touched his meat to hers. "We can talk more about this after dinner. What's going on at the shop that kept you late?"

As they ate, Mary brought Ron up to date on business growth and how more diverse clients were coming in. She watched his reaction when she mentioned the growing number of quinceanera parties and first communions, along with a growing number of Asians and African-Americans asking about catering.

"The business grows more. Depending on cuisine requests and needs, we may be hiring or contracting out work." Ron laid his fork and knife down, wiped his mouth, and pushed his plate aside. "More than what I could finish."

"I thought about that, too. Jeff's input is important." Mary pushed back from the table some. "I like that Cascade Bay is growing and becoming more diverse. It's not a small town anymore."

"Last city council meeting, a few brought up applying for city status with Sacramento. It'll be interesting to watch how things change and adapt. Most of all, new cuisines and recipes to try and learn." Ron reached for the check their server had left on the table earlier.

Mary put her hand on part of the check. "Megallions is still open. You buying ice cream or am I?"

"Thanks for the offer. I'm too full." Ron tugged the check out from under Mary's hand.

"I am, too. I was going to get mine to go if we did." Mary put her napkin on the table and stood up.

Ron rose, came around the table, and reached for Mary's hand. "We'll rain check it for now. I've enjoyed our conversation and dinner."

Mary squeezed his hand. "I did, too. I'll wait until we're outside to say more."

Ron nodded, led them through the dining room out to the main entrance. He paid the check and held the door open for Mary. Outside, he paused by one of the benches. "Sit down. We can talk more."

Mary shook her head, looking at her watch. "It's after eight. Carena's first full day is tomorrow. Order is coming in, too. What I've got to say won't take long."

"Sure. Go ahead." Ron faced her.

She leaned in and whispered, "I'm still not sure about doing three-way nude cuddles. My curiosity wants to know more. For now, I'm going to think about it and let you know."

Ron pulled back, gave her a hot up and down look. Grinning, he shot her a thumbs up and closed the space between them. He slipped an arm around her waist and hugged her tight to him. There was no mistaking how what she said affected Ron. The hot, passionate French kiss went on for several moments until a car full of teens honked their horn as they drove by, calling out, "Get a room!"

Mary broke off the kiss, moving a couple of steps back. "Wow! I know your thoughts on three-way cuddles."

Ron laughed. "I'm intrigued. Three-way cuddles work for some. I've had my share. I don't have to have them. One-on-one loving works fine for me, too."

"Thank you. I appreciate your honesty. Walk me to my car?" Mary took her keys out of her purse.

"You bet. Usual text we're each home, okay?" Ron checked the back seat of her car as she opened the door and the interior lights came on. "Want me to follow you home?"

"Not necessary. Darcey is home. I'll text as soon as I'm inside." She kissed Ron's cheek and got in. She watched him get in his car and flash the headlights he was in safely. Five minutes later, she was on the interstate heading home.

Tonight's discussion was awkward, yet, they both took a chance on admitting their feelings. She still had reservations about three-way cuddles. Talking with Jeff would take a few days to find the time as each of them would be occupied with work.

Ron exited Ranagian's parking lot shortly after Mary. He followed her until she entered the interstate taking her south then east. He turned at the next light onto Lakeshore Boulevard. He put his Bluetooth earpiece on as he waited for the left turn arrow to enter East-West Highway bypass to avoid the north-south interstate traffic. As the arrow came on, Jeff answered his phone.

"Hey, Ron," Jeff said. "Let me put you on speaker."

"Go ahead. I've got you on Bluetooth." Ron changed lanes, moving into the high-speed lane and set the cruise control.

"Thanks. You got my text, yes?" Jeff asked.

"I did. Mary and I had dinner and talked about it."

"What?" Jeff asked in a loud, squeaky voice.

Ron could hear him clearing his throat several times. There was no mistaking his surprise. "I let her know you texted me. Shared the text, too. *After* we had talked about why she's curious. Better she knows we're talking than not."

"I guess. I mean, what if I wanted this between you and me only?" Jeff's exasperated sigh rumbled out of the phone.

"You gotta speak up. This isn't something that affects only you and me. It's about all three of us. These things have to be out in the open. Trust and consent are central." Ron reached over and adjusted the phone's volume.

"Yeah, I know. I'm trying to wrap my head around all of this and still be in on things. Do I owe either of you an apology?"

"Nah," Ron replied. "Mary and I are extroverts. You're introverted. We have to keep in mind you don't think out loud or process via verbal discourse the way we do. Nothing wrong with that."

"Whew," Jeff said. He didn't say anything more.

"You still there?" Ron turned the cruise control off and slowed to change lanes. The sign he passed said two miles to his exit.

"Yeah. Just thinking." Jeff's yawn followed. "Sorry. Been a long day."

"I know that feeling. Was there something you needed to talk about tonight?" Ron asked, exiting the highway.

"Just how to approach talking about Mary's curiosity. I'm not good at being obvious." Jeff chuckled and added, "Well, being obviously transparent."

"Maybe you need to set a time to talk about it. Kinda make a date. We talked over dinner. Setting limited how much we said." Ron turned onto his street.

"How come you're so good at this?" Jeff yawned again.

"Good at what?" Ron asked, turning into his driveway.

"Knowing what to do? What to say?"

"Oh, practice I guess." Ron chuckled. "Seriously, a lot of relationship stuff is try and try again. Errors happen. It gives you learning curves and knowledge. I'm not an expert."

"Guess it's like Susan asking me to help out with interviewing chefs and the business side of her new restaurant. I got the experience and know-how. I can pass that on to her," Jeff sleepily said.

"You got it, bro. Listen, you're beat. I'm home and need Zs myself." Ron yawned. "Let's call it a night."

"Agreed. Sleep well. Talk later." Jeff hung up.

Ron pulled into the garage, shut the car off, disconnected his Bluetooth earpiece, and texted Mary. As he closed the garage, his cell phone beeped. He glanced at it as he locked up and set the house alarm. He grinned. Mary's response to his text read: *Home safe. Good sleep.*

Ron smiled as he climbed the stairs to his bedroom. Sometimes life brought what you least expected. Tonight was one of those times. Mary's curiosity and intellect gifted them with a stimulating dinner conversation. They learned something about each other. Mary opened herself to new information. He gained a better understanding of how her mind worked. With Jeff, he wanted help, too. All of them did in some fashion, and they each got it whether they said it or not. As he undressed, Ron smiled more. Peace filled him. A relaxing contentment knowing that the three of them had reached out to the other not only because they trusted. They felt safe and secure, too.

He set the alarm, turned out the light, and pulled the sheet over him. His last thought as sleep claimed him was the acceptance and comfort his developing triad provided him.

Chapter Twelve

Sacramento, Three Days Later-Late Afternoon

Jeff shut his computer down and pushed back from the hotel room's desk. He'd hit the ground running. Susan had lined up interviews the afternoon he'd arrived. Two candidates stood out. One was a former top chef from a restaurant in Chicago who wanted a lower-key job with fewer responsibilities. The other had less tenure running an haute cuisine restaurant. His references and referrals came from several top chefs in San Francisco and Los Angeles. Susan's earlier call about offering both the candidates the job might be the optimal option she was looking for. A person with the experience to create the dishes and oversee the kitchen staff with an assistant who would handle production, purchasing, and some of the cooking. Two chefs working in tandem to oversee the premiere of one of Sacramento's nouvelle restaurants—he liked the idea. Tomorrow, he and Susan along with Tim would meet with the two candidates and make them an offer.

Tonight, he wanted to relax and get lost in the thoughts running through his head since he'd listened to Ron's voicemail earlier. Building two relationships simultaneously took focus he hadn't considered before. Rebuilding his and Mary's and working through what the hell a polyamorous one with Ron looked like baffled him. Ron's suggestion the two of them talk without Mary around made sense. Jeff glanced at his watch. Two hours until Ron would call back. Time to grab a bite to eat and scribble down some of the phrases and questions that came back to him each time he thought about an open relationship and relationships in general.

Two distinct knocks rattled the room door. A voice called out, "Room service, sir."

Jeff made his way across the room, noting where his briefcase and portfolio were. "One moment, please."

As he unlocked the door, he glanced over his shoulder. The late afternoon sun beat down on the room's external patio. Last check the outdoor thermometer read one-hundred-and-six degrees. The latest weather report joked of a nighttime low of ninety-five. No rain in sight for the next week. How Tim and Susan lived with such weather, he didn't know. They didn't blink an eye at the bills and costs Susan shared concerning the restaurant. Tim smiled and nodded when she said he backed her a hundred percent on the venture. And a six-bedroom house with a pool...talk about expense and upkeep. Tim offered a piece of advice about investing wisely and fixing up a house with a great location and potential.

"Thank you, sir," the server said, pushing the cart holding his dinner into the room. "Your wine is on the second shelf in a pitcher surrounded by ice. A pot of tea, cream, and sugar are on that shelf, as well."

Jeff pointed to the desk. "Over there, please."

"Very good, sir." The server pushed the cart close to the desk, turned, and lifted the lid off the plate on the top shelf. "Your steak medium rare with sautéed baby red potatoes with basil, thyme, and tomatoes."

The server set the cover on the desk. She leaned down, took a small tray off the bottom shelf of the cart, and set it next to the plate. "Your dinner salad with croutons and feta cheese. Honey mustard dressing is in the container next to the dinner rolls and butter."

Jeff inhaled. His mouth salivated as his stomach growled. The server chuckled and smiled as he glanced at her. "I'll be sure to let Chef Stone know your stomach and nose agree with his aroma choices."

Jeff snickered. "Tell Stone he's still got the touch when it comes to presentation and aroma. Let him know Jeff from culinary school thanks him for preparing this."

"I shall, sir." The server set the rest of the order on the desk along with the main course and utensils. As she straightened, she held another plate. "This is a new dessert that Chef Stone is offering free with each meal. Strawberry-Cherry Red Velvet Cake. Shall I leave it with you?"

Jeff looked at the medium-sized piece of cake covered with a deep red frosting, bits of strawberries and cherries. The cake looked fluffy and ready to send anyone's taste buds to nirvana and back. "Leave it and the cart, please. I'll put it out in the hall and call down when I'm done."

"Fine, sir. Please sign the receipt." The server held out the slip with his order on it.

Jeff signed, handed the slip back, and relocked the door after the server exited. Within a few moments, he had space cleared on the desk to set his dinner and wine glass. He opened one of the two small bottles chilling amongst the ice in the small pitcher. A crisp, full bouquet greeted him as he passed the bottle beneath his nose. Hints of pears, apples, and cherries mixed tighter as he sipped the wine between bites of steak or salad. Stone had once again outdone himself with the steak. Cracked pepper with slivers of garlic and a slight tang of lemon graced each bite. The steak was cooked to perfection. So tender it could be cut with a butter knife even though he used a steak knife.

Jeff rose, walked over to the bed, and picked up his portfolio. He opened it to the legal pad inside. On the pad, he'd written down several words that kept coming to mind as he thought about polyamory. His online research yielded that the common agreed-upon definition was many loves. Some called it responsible non-monogamy. Others referred to it as open relationships. The harbingers of polyamory's wrongness labeled it uncommitted with a focus solely on sex. Jeff smiled as he sat back down. The more he read, the more he didn't agree with the harbingers. Feelings mattered, people mattered, and so did relationships along with families. Why did he feel uneasy about the aspect of polyamory then?

He picked up a pen and looked at the list he'd started last night about this. His first reason read it was new and different. He got that. Number two was more of a question than a statement. How did he know he could be successful at poly? Below it he'd written, 'Only by trying. And talking things out.' Number three had him grinning again. It backed up his response to number two—Communicate, communicate, communicate. The blasted poly mantra that popped up under most Q-and-A advice sections he found. Did he have a fourth reason? Or a fifth? Were there objections or uncertainties that came with doing something new?

He laid the pen down, picked up his wine glass, swirled the contents around, and sipped. He wasn't sure how many minutes passed while he finished his wine and stared at the list. Smirking, he set the glass down, picked up the pen, and crossed out the list's title. He didn't have ten reasons against poly. Concerns, yes. Questions, yes. He jotted a few words and partial questions to talk over with Ron. For now, his dinner was getting cold. Steak deserved appreciation while it remained warm and appealing.

Jeff flipped through the local travel magazine the desk clerk had given him upon check-in as he ate. The review section talked about upcoming new businesses. Susan's interview was included. Haute Nouvelle was set to open in ninety days. The interview talked about offering local cuisine with an upscale flair and atmosphere. If Susan's plan worked out, she planned to open Haute Nouvelle II in Cascade Bay early next year. She and Tim had dropped hints about him overseeing it. He wasn't sure beyond offering some financial backing. It depended on how well his European ventures panned out. Ona was due to call with a report next month. Jeff finished eating and poured a mug of tea when his cell phone rang. Caller id showed Ron's number.

He stirred his tea as he answered. "Hey, Ron. Hold on a sec. Let me put you on speaker."

"Okay."

"Thanks. I'm finishing up dinner. Might be slow to answer." Jeff forked a bite of cake into his mouth. Sugary sweetness mixed with the fruit tartness slid across his taste buds. Damn, Stone was on to something with this dessert.

"No problem. I'm patient remember." Ron's chuckle rushed out of the speaker.

Jeff swallowed and countered, "Patient to a point if I remember correctly."

Ron's laughter sounded again, followed by a few coughs. "Possibly true. Another subject for another chat."

Jeff chortled. "I'll put it on my calendar with a reminder for twenty years from now."

"Sounds good. Back to why I called?"

Jeff pressed his lips together, cupped his tea mug tighter, and looked at his list. One of the top questions he jotted down, underlined, and boxed stood out. Did he have to bare his soul constantly? Keeping stuff inside got him through a lot. Was that going to have to change to be poly?

He set the mug down, pulled the phone closer, and replied, "Sure."

Ron didn't speak for a few moments. Jeff turned his phone over to make sure they were still connected. He wet his lips, ready to speak when Ron spoke.

"How do you feel about Mary and me?"

Jeff rocked back in his chair. Talk about a direct question. That wasn't one he'd anticipated. Under his top question, the first response said, 'Don't lie, be as truthful as you can.' "Best I can put it in words. Uncertain. Too new to say?"

"I get it. It took me by surprise, too."

Jeff gathered his dishes and placed them on the cart. "How?"

"Mary and I knew each other from a couple of weddings we worked before you two got together."

"Okay." Jeff sat back down and nibbled at the remaining third of the piece of cake. "Had your eye on her for a while?"

"Appreciating a nice woman and a good-looking one, too. Nothing more." Ron's tone changed as he continued. *"Poly doesn't equate promiscuous."*

Jeff leaned back in the chair. What had he said to ignite that reaction? "What'd I say?"

"Sorry. Hot topic for me. Got razzed about chasing women rather than settling down."

"Didn't know this. Mary's a looker. It took me a while to ask her out."

Ron's breathy *uh-huh* rattle the speaker. Jeff took the phone off speaker and held it to his ear. "I'm researching poly. Finding lots of info. Lots of contradictions, too."

"I've heard poly described as many different versions available for sampling. I found what appealed to me."

"Read about lots of trial and error, too." Jeff put his mug and dessert plate on the cart. He picked up his portfolio and pen, walked to the bed, and sat down. He kicked his shoes off, propped two pillows against the headboard, and leaned back on them. "Are you okay with Mary and me?"

"Be less than truthful if I said sure. Been a while since I pursued a primary relationship."

"Primary?" Jeff flipped open his portfolio and grabbed his pen. This needed noting. He'd still didn't get layered relationships.

"A kind of ranking. Nana Rose calls her boyfriend her main squeeze."

"Is that necessary?" Jeff sunk lower into the pillows behind him.

"Depends on what you want and those involved want."

"Okay. Back to you about Mary and me. Your thoughts?"

"We've been friends for a long time. I trust you in many ways." Ron stopped talking.

"But?" Jeff started to sit up.

"Just like you, it's new and different for me, too. Been a secondary many times over."

"Ah, the other boyfriend."

Ron's weak laugh had Jeff ready to sit upright when Ron said, "Now I'm looking for someone to live with. Share finances. Make a home with."

"Even if it includes another guy or family members?"

"Yes," Ron answered, his voice strong and vibrant. "I like the idea of a shared household and lots of love going on. You?"

"Ten months ago, I'd have said you were nuts. And said no way."

"And now?"

Jeff grinned as he laid his pen and portfolio on the bedside table. "I'm learning. Seeing different ways to do family. And some of it intrigues me."

"Are you in?"

"I don't want to hurt Mary again. I want her in my life."

"Me too," Ron said.

"I guess that means we're going to give this a try."

"Sounds like it."

Jeff and Ron continued their conversation a few minutes longer. Jeff started yawning when Ron said, "We need to talk to Mary, too."

"Yes, we do. For now, I need to sleep." Jeff stood, pulled the curtains closed as he bid Ron goodnight, and ended the call. Jeff was halfway back to the bed when he realized Ron's last statement was about seeing Mary a couple of times while he was in Sacramento.

Buzz! Buzz! Jeff looked down at his phone. It showed two messages waiting. He saw texts from Ron and Mary. He opened Ron's first.

FYI so you don't freak on my last stmt. Mary & I
are having dinner w/my sis Abebi 1 night. Seeing a
movie with Darcey and Lindsay another. We'll be
well chaperoned!

Jeff snorted. Read the text again and burst out laughing. Having a three-year-old and a four-and-a-half-year-old along might not fit the strict definition of a chaperone. If Tabitha was even a bit like Lindsay, Ron and Mary were in for a busy couple of evenings.

Jeff read Mary's text next. She wished him a pleasant, dream-filled sleep. Lindsay missed him, too, and said night-night. Mary's last line ignited his smile and kept him smiling as he stripped down to his briefs. He tossed his clothes on the chair next to the bed. He picked up his phone as he lay in the bed, rereading Mary's message. Mary and her heart missed him. It wasn't a love declaration. It was a simple *I care* message that came from her heart. He sent a brief reply saying he and his heart missed her. He added a postscript to hug Lindsay goodnight for him. Mary's reply came through before he plugged in his phone to charge. It read "done" and had his name in between a double set of parentheses. He found the emoticon he wanted and sent it.

One yawn followed by another indicated sleep wasn't far off. His last thought as he turned out the light and pulled the sheet over him focused on the three of them communicating well. Maybe they might make this poly configuration called a triad work.

Chapter Thirteen

Mary leaned back against her pillows, smiling as she read Jeff's reply to her last text. A smiley face with heart eyes and blowing a kiss. Caring was definitely happening. Even Ron had sent her a lovey-dovey-eyed emoticon earlier in the day. To say neither man held a special place in her heart would be an outright lie. One that she couldn't deny unless she wanted to lie to herself. Did caring mean the same as loving? Did one equal the other all the time? For some, it did. Risking her heart was something she hadn't consciously done since Warren. Jeff had gotten close and even pulled her into a relationship that she had planned to be friends with benefits only. Had she lost control over her instincts? Somehow missed the signals her gut and heart usually sent her?

Or were you too busy guarding the outside to know what your heart needed and wanted?

Great, the one question her therapist had asked more than once during their weekly sessions right after Jeff left. Dr. Sharon Saxon didn't mince advice or play games when asking pertinent questions. Sharon had hit close to home with that question. Mary wondered if she dared ponder it beyond a superficial aspect until she talked with Ron and Jeff more. Even let her mind go into the what-if questions Sharon suggested she think over when Jeff had first asked her out.

A soft knock sounded against the bedroom door. Mary looked up as the door opened.

"Mom, are you still awake?" Darcey asked, her voice laced with tears.

"Yes. Come in." Mary patted the bed. "Sit down. What's up?"

Darcey sat on the bed close to her. "I thought I'd let go of the pain Zeke's walking out caused."

Mary nodded. "Breakups can be hard. It's not easy moving past the pain and regret."

Darcey sighed, sniffled, and looked down. "That was three years ago. Why am I feeling like it just happened?"

Mary laid her hand on top of Darcey's and squeezed. "Pain can etch its way into parts of us we don't know about. Remember what Sharon said about guarding our exterior thinking we were guarding our hearts at the same time?"

"Yes."

"I think we haven't listened to what our hearts need and want very well." Mary handed Darcey a tissue. "What do we do?"

Darcey plucked pieces off the tissue, dropping them on the bed. Mary knew she wasn't paying attention to what she was doing. Darcey shredded things when she needed emotional release.

Darcey finally looked up. "Talk about what our hearts are telling our heads."

Mary smiled, nodding. "Yes. Each of us has some communicating with ourselves we need to do. Sometimes saying things aloud breaks down the barrier. Shall I go first?"

"I think I want to go first." Darcey cleared her throat and continued, "I worry about spending the rest of my life alone. I mean, without a partner, a life partner. Lindsay is growing up fast. Going to pre-school in a year. Yet Zeke refuses to take on joint custody. He wants visitation without having to deal with raising her."

Darcey paused, looking at her. Mary nodded. "You're worried about being alone, lack of life partner, and Zeke continuing to be a dick bag over his own kid."

"Good summation." Darcey winked as she added, "Lindsay deserves a father who wants to be in her life, not just when it's convenient."

"Agreed. What else?"

"Well..." Darcey's voice trailed off. She looked at Mary like she wanted to say more but wasn't sure.

"Darcey, what is it? You know you can tell me anything." Mary started to reach out to Darcey.

Darcey held up her hand and blurted out, "Jaxson asked me out, and then Nathan did."

Mary swallowed, counting to twenty by twos. Darcey had come home later than expected from talking with Jaxson and Nathan about carpooling schedules over pizza. She hadn't said much more than carpooling talk had gone down. Mary wet her lips and asked, "Both at same time or separately?"

"Separately at first. I said I needed to think about it. Nathan brought it up again at dinner. Jaxson seconded the idea and added together and separately worked for him."

Mary pressed her lips together. Had more of Cascade Bay turned polyamorous? What did Ron know about this? She opened her mouth, ready to tell Darcey about Ron and Jeff, when Darcey spoke again.

"I like Jaxson and Nathan. I'm attracted to them, too. Is it wrong to want to date both of them at the same time? They called tonight our first group date."

Mary turned, facing Darcey straight on. "No, it's not. Consent matters. I'm doing the same thing with Jeff and Ron."

Darcey gasped, gawking at her wide-eyed. "*You're what?*"

"No TMI exclamations either." Mary pointed at Darcey. "We're going through the same thing."

Darcey nodded. "What are *we* going to do about it?"

"I'm seeing Jeff and Ron together and separately. We're talking about what works for us. Ron says we're pursuing a polyamorous relationship."

Darcey looked away and back at her. Mary nodded and added, "If that's what you want to try with Jaxson and Nathan, go for it. Only the three of you can decide what's right for you."

"Yeah, but..."

"But what, Darcey?" Mary asked.

"What about Lindsay? What if Zeke finds out?"

"There's a lot of what-ifs. What if you want to be happy, and Lindsay thrives because of this? Zeke can't do shit without going to court, and you know what the judge said at your divorce hearing."

"If he wanted visitation, he had to live locally because a three-year-old doesn't understand their main parent not being close by if they want them."

"Right, and the psychologist agreed with him, as did his social worker. Has he moved back or even hinted at this?"

"No."

"Then stop worrying. Go for what you want, and your heart tells you is right for you."

"Shouldn't you be doing the same thing?"

"I think I am."

"Really. Aren't we needing to risk our hearts and dare to love again?"

Mary sighed. "I think that is happening whether we realize it or not."

"Maybe for you. I can't say yet. I just had my first group date."

"Here's my worries, short and sweet. Then we sleep. We'll talk more over breakfast." Mary yawned. "Being hurt, things not working out, and never done this before."

"Who knew we'd end up in the same relationship configuration?" Darcey asked, standing up.

"Life hands us what we're ready for, according to Sharon. Maybe we're each ready for a new phase of life. Seeing and trying things that put us outside our comfort zones."

"I think I'll call Sharon in the morning. I need to talk this out more." Darcey leaned down and hugged her. "Thanks, Mom. I love you."

Mary hugged Darcey tightly. She let go as she said, "Love you, too. Sleep well."

"I think I will," Darcey said before closing the bedroom door.

Mary turned out the light and pulled the sheet up. She slid down into her pillows until she found a comfortable position. Sleep didn't come for a few minutes longer. A lot of revelation happened in the space of their hour-long talk. What came next, Mary wasn't sure. Maybe Ron might have some resources she could point Darcey to. Mary yawned again and snuggled deeper into her pillow and covers. Sleep would either yield dreams of explanation or more weird ones like she'd had the last few nights about a consensual three-way cuddle with Ron and Jeff. Ones she'd have to discuss with Sharon when they next had lunch.

TWO DAYS LATER

Mary waved at Sharon as she walked across the restaurant patio toward her. She waited until Sharon got close to the table to greet her. "Hi. Thanks for inking me in on short notice."

Sharon smiled, put her purse on the table, and pulled out the chair opposite Mary. "Two hours open permits time for a leisure lunch and talking."

"It does. I'm glad you're here." Mary picked up the menu. "Le Chardon's salads are awesome. Their open-face sliced pot roast sandwiches are totally worth killing your calorie count."

Sharon chuckled. "I think I know what I'm having." She pointed to the specials. "Sliced pot roast on a fresh mixed bed of greens with caramelized onions and dressing choice, topped with mixed shredded cheese."

Mary grinned as the server approached. "I think that we've made up our minds. How about some of the mixed fresh fruit and yogurt to go with it?"

"Sounds awesome." Sharon handed their menus to the server, who quickly took their order.

"I'll put this in and be back with your lemon waters." The server walked off.

"What is up?" Sharon asked, turning more toward her. "You sounded worried when you called."

"I am and I'm not. I know that doesn't make sense." Mary toyed with her napkin. She rolled up the loose top edge and unrolled it twice before looking up.

"It does make sense if you're unsure about something. Dealing with unknowns isn't the way logic works. It deals in knowns." Sharon took her silverware out of her napkin and smoothed the napkin across her lap.

"There's a lot of unknowns mixed with the few things I do." Mary waited until the server left again before saying more. She picked up her water, drank and sat the glass down. "How familiar are you with the term polyamory?"

"Heard of it. Basic meaning is many loves. Why?" Sharon laid her hands on the table.

"I'm seeing Jeff again and Ron, too." Mary laid her napkin on her lap, picked up her fork, ready to eat the salad the server sat in front of her.

"Thank you," Sharon said and cut into her salad. She didn't speak until the server refilled their water glasses and walked away. "Okay. Do Jeff and Ron know?"

"Yes. We've talked about it all together and some individually." Mary ate and chewed, waiting for Sharon's reply.

"You're trying to rebuild yours and Jeff's relationship at the same time?"

"Yes, we are."

Sharon put her fork down. She folded her hands together, steepled her fingers, and tapped them against her lips for several moments. Mary continued eating. Chewing slowly as more questions and concerns flooded her mind. Was Sharon staying quiet waiting for her to say more like she had in some of their prior discussions? Or weighing the pros and cons of what was said?

"Is this fair to everyone? Are you trying to build two relationships at once?"

"Good question, Sharon. One that I've asked myself a few times. Ron and Jeff both say they're fine with it. At times I'm okay with it."

"What's the problem?" Sharon picked up her fork and pointed it at Mary and said. "Not what you think I or anybody else wants to hear. What is your *issue* with this?"

"Wow. To the point as always." Mary stared at Sharon. She could cut to the core on things. Sharon nodded and kept on eating.

Mary finished her salad, drank some water, and wiped her mouth. She looked away, out over the beach and bay. Waves rolled in at varying levels and intensity, breaking across the beach. Then sweeping back out, leaving new patterns in the sand. The water appeared to smooth out only to rise and roll in again, splashing along the beach up against those walking close to the shoreline or rock formations further out at the edge of the bay. Her life resembled the chaos that churned beneath the waters from time to time. Other times it was the smooth, calm top layer that permeated other aspects. Where did the two meet? The mix found a compromise that all could live with? The key answer was a mix she could live with and still flex when she needed to. That part she couldn't answer.

Mary looked back at Sharon. "I deal with knowns and repeat business day in and day out."

"Right." Sharon set her empty salad plate aside and pulled one of the fruit and yogurt plates to her.

"Trial and error upset the balance that has become my life. My way of doing things." Mary speared a piece of fruit and popped it into her mouth.

"Haven't you upset that with what you're already doing? Dating Jeff, rebuilding with him, and doing similar with Ron?" Sharon dipped a strawberry chunk into her yogurt.

Mary ate more of her fruit, wiped her fingers on her napkin, and finished her water. "Good comeback. I've changed, yet I want sameness around me. Some tether point to hang on to so it all makes sense."

Sharon smirked. "Honey, we all do. You're not unique in that desire. It's how you find it that differs for each of us. Mine is knowing my inner strengths and when to ask for help. It doesn't always work out smoothly."

"You have weak areas?" Mary quipped, smiling.

Sharon laughed. "First thing a good therapist admits. Doesn't let it on to her patients like I just did. But you're a friend, so I can dare some vulnerability."

"Thanks. I'll..." Mary began as Sharon's phone rang.

Sharon picked her phone up, glanced at the caller id. "It's the answering service. I'll be back in a moment."

Sharon rose and walked away from the table a short distance.

"Will there be anything else, ma'am?" the server asked, holding their bill.

"We're done." Mary reached for the bill. "Thank you."

"You're welcome. Let me know if you need anything else." The server handed her the bill and left.

Sharon walked back to the table, shaking her head. "Sorry. I've got to run. A client is waiting for me at the office. The service forgot to tell me about the appointment this morning."

"No problem. I'll get the check. Figure it covers the cost of the session." Mary rose and walked around the table, opening her arms. Sharon moved toward her, opening her arms too. They embraced and separated.

"This is one of those 'roll with' things I mentioned. My receptionist is on vacation until Monday. I'm dealing with temp help and some days it's me and the service fielding calls and billing issues." Sharon picked up her purse. "Call me if you need to talk more. But wait till next week."

Mary laughed. "Right. I'll tell Darcey to call you next week then."

"She already called me this morning. Don't ask about what. Client therapist privilege, you know." Sharon waved and exited the patio through the street entrance.

Mary slung her purse over her shoulder, picked up the check, and headed into the lobby to pay. Good, Darcey had contacted Sharon already. That lifted a few items off her list of worries. Talking with Sharon had shed light in areas that needed further thought. Thought that also needed conversation and input from Jeff and Ron. Problem was, Jeff wouldn't be back for four more days. She could talk to Ron tomorrow night after their dinner with Abebi.

Chapter Fourteen

Two Days Later

Mary sat down at her kitchen table. The pad with the notes from her and Darcey's latest discussion lay on the table next to her. A new notebook lay next to it. A red pen and blue one lay between the pads. Sharon suggested journaling about any thoughts or questions that came up after she talked with Ron or Jeff.

Phone calls with Jeff hadn't panned out since he was either in meetings with Susan and the two new chefs she'd hired, or he was busy with his investment broker and lawyers working on Ona buying out his portion of two of the restaurants they jointly owned. In one of their quick scant conversations, he mentioned he was glad Ona decided to take on sole ownership of the two burgeoning restaurants. She had come up with the ideas and ran with them from the start. He only invested in them because his dad's estate hadn't finished settling at the time. Now Ona could buy him out and he wouldn't have to worry about the Europe half of his financial investments as much.

Ron had made time to talk and see her a day after their dinner with Abebi and Tabitha. Otherwise, they'd never gotten time to talk. Movie night had turned into a fiasco with Lindsay and Tabitha melting down as they stood in line for the opening night of a new kid's film. Popcorn and cartoon reruns at his place with Chinese takeout didn't offer a chance to do more than hold hands, steal a few kisses, and stare at each other adoringly.

She flipped back the top two pages of the pad, past the lists she and Darcey had made. Past her scribbles on what she remembered from her thoughts as she and Sharon talked. The page she stopped on was the one with her notes on polyamory. The definitions and comments that struck her as she combed the internet reading different sources and articles. Some sent chills racing down her back, making her wonder if she'd gone off the deep end even contemplating trying this out. The quote she'd drawn a square around and underlined twice resonated with her more than anything else. It summed up taking a leap of faith.

Flying in the face of your greatest fear and acknowledging why it scared you shitless. Boy, did that hit the nail on the head for her.

One other item stood out on the page. It defined how she felt about the small amount she knew about poly and what it meant to go a different path. A famous ice cream parlor offered a vast array of flavors and combinations of flavors mixed together. They encouraged all comers to try and come up with their own original mix. Well, she was doing that. Going down her own path and finding what worked for her. Maybe two guys were safer than one, or it was the thrill of having two want and desire her. See her as a sexual woman still in her prime.

What did this all boil down to? Was it all just about sex and doing it again until it got old and boring? Let things run their course and when it started to fade, walk away? She might have in the past. Prior to Jeff leaving, there was that potential. She hadn't registered her fear, her uncertainty, or her own needs and desires. These days she knew herself better and with a deeper appreciation of where she came from and where she might be going.

Mary turned to the next page and grinned. Ten questions stood out of the myriad of partial ones she'd jotted down. First, she needed to know what Jeff or Ron expected from her and the relationship. What were their needs and wants? The last ones covered her internal thoughts and quirks. Risking her heart scared her. Love made you vulnerable and open to a lot of risk. A lot of pain and a lot of joy. Warren had wanted to be her everything. He pouted when she went out with her friends or asked for space to do things with Darcey even though he encouraged her to do things on her own. He wanted and needed family. He expected her to want the same. Talk about dichotomy. Hindsight showed she hadn't wanted the same thing Warren had on many small items because she hadn't known how to say no or talk about what she wanted. Now she did.

Ron had hinted at alone time and space for each of them. He took notes during their dinnertime talk while Abebi bathed Tabitha. His key item was about making time for each couple to have space to date and relate without triangling all the time and a go-ahead from each of them. He laughed when she asked about him and Jeff hanging out. Ron said that might be and it might not. It was a guy thing that they would have to work out. He turned his pad over when she tried to look at it. He grinned, blew her a kiss, and said he wrote in shorthand too much like a doctor for anyone else to understand it right then.

Was he hiding something? Not saying what he really felt? Past experiences were cropping up again based on other guys and not Ron's experiences, which she really didn't have.

Mary picked up the pen and turned to a blank page, speaking as she wrote. "I believe love exists for everyone. I'm not sure what that looks like right now. I'm scared based on my past. Poly is so different. So full of what-ifs and having to trust me, Ron, and Jeff to be truthful and honest. Am I in, or am I out?"

She paused, tapping the pad with the pen. Did she have to declare love to be in or could she say yes, let's see where this goes and let love happen on its own? The more she silently repeated that to herself, the calmer she got. There was an empowering aspect to living in the moment and caring about the guys freely without having to hide or choose one over the other. Her main question changed. Could the three of them decide on what their poly configuration looked like?

Ron rinsed the last plate, handed it to Abebi, and dried his hands on the extra dishtowel on the rack near the kitchen window. He turned and flipped the electric teakettle on. "What flavor tea tonight?"

Abebi put the plate in the cabinet closest to her. "How about honey and lemon?"

Ron set two cups on the counter and placed a tea bag in each. "Sounds good. Nana Rose called me."

"Oh?" Abebi hung the towel she had on the rack next to the other. "Is she checking up on you again?"

"No, checking up on you. She's worried. You haven't returned her calls."

"Yes, I know. Between work, school, and Tabitha, I don't have a lot of free time. Then there's..." Abebi's voice trailed off. She looked down and back up at him.

Ron nodded. "It's not like I don't know. Jess came into the diner yesterday for lunch asking if I could give him your number."

Abebi winced. Ron started to reach out to her. She shied away, shrugging. "Well—er-er...there's..."

"Sis, stop with the *there's* line. What's going on?"

Abebi walked over to the table, pulled out a chair and sat down. She turned the chair, facing him as she spoke. "I'm seeing Mack, too."

Ron held up two fingers. He was sure his lips moved like a fish out of water. His sister, who hadn't seriously dated since high school, was seeing two men. Most of her flings were with women. Her two-year stint with the woman who walked out on Abebi—after she'd found out she was pregnant after a one-night stand—was the longest affair she'd had. He licked his lips, shook his head, and pointed at Abebi. "Two guys? At the same time?"

Abebi nodded, giving him a weak grin.

"You sure about this?" he asked, standing next to Abebi.

"As sure as you are about Jeff and Mary."

The kettle started to whistle. Ron replied as he made their tea. "I never said I was sure. I think we've got a chance to make it work."

"If you aren't sure, why go for it? Do it?" Abebi took her mug from him, added a dab of honey, and stirred.

"Life carries very few certainties. Birth, death, and taxes are non-negotiable certainties as Grandpa Jack was fond of saying. In between, that is where chaos and uncertainty mix a lot." He sat across from Abebi, picked up his mug, blew on the hot contents, and sipped. "There's one other thing that makes me cautious."

"Okay. That word *there* seems to be faving our conversation." Abebi sipped her tea. "What else has you spooked?"

Ron laid his hands on the table near his open laptop, inhaled, and slowly exhaled. "Velma."

Abebi rocked back, her eyes widened. "Velma? After all this time? Really?"

Ron nodded, trying to smile, but all he could manage was a weak grin. "Oh yes. She and Ed wanted *more* than any one person could give."

"Ouch," Abebi responded. "She's the one who told you you were a shitty lover."

"Yes. That doesn't sting anymore. The exclusivity demand mixed with their control freak needs..." Ron wrapped his hands around his mug, letting the warmth seep into them. "They wanted a submissive instead of a partner."

Abebi laid her hand on his arm. "They're the ones who didn't want you at Tabitha's birth. *Bitch*."

Ron shook his head. "To each their own. They had issues they needed to work out before they opened the relationship. Not the other way around."

"I'm sorry you're still skittish. I've watched your other relationships and learned that each is unique."

"Thanks. Took a while to separate the bad stuff from the good. It's easier when you don't doubt yourself."

Abebi raised her mug, saying, "Here's to good relationships. Taking care and never doubting us again."

Ron tapped his mug against Abebi's, swallowed a third of the cooled tea, and set the mug down. "I agree. Are you ready to tackle two guys at once?"

Abebi ducked her head and came up grinning from ear to ear. "Oh yeah. Jess can kiss and—Mack, well, he can—"

Ron held up one hand, calling out, "TMI! TMI! You're my sister. I don't need to know all those details."

Abebi laughed. "I want a relationship. Someone who is there for Tabitha and me. Jess and Mack adore her. She likes them. Why not give it a shot?"

Ron rose, picked up their mugs, and set them in the sink. He turned, leaning against the counter. "Same way I feel about Mary. Jeff's got his good points and he's a friend. My gut says trust and follow your heart."

"Momma," Tabitha yelled. "I'm done with my bath."

Abebi rose. "I better go get her. She'll streak soaking wet through the house again if I don't."

Ron chuckled. "Yes, our little nudist. Not a prude, for sure."

As Abebi started to exit the kitchen, he added, "Sis, take time to figure out what you each want and communicate that. It matters."

Abebi turned back, nodding. "For sure. We'll talk more. I'm gonna have questions and need advice."

Advice? He could talk about pitfalls and errors. How about the good side of poly? The joys. The extra love and support that came from caring for and being cared for. Love that multiplied and sometimes grew. Sometimes it stagnated like monogamous relationships did. Ron sat down at the table and pulled his laptop to him. He opened his password-protected journal to his last entry. He read it twice before adding to it.

What does poly mean to me? More love, more people around, a network of friends and lovers that forms a family nucleus that adds on to your birth family. It can include sex and often does. It means risk, being vulnerable, and taking a chance. It embraces hearing everyone out and making decisions that affect all three of us together.

He saved the entry, shut down his laptop, and exited the kitchen. Tabitha was waiting for her nightly story. Abebi, too, since he started the three-way storytelling. Tonight, Tabitha got to start the story, Abebi got the middle, and his part was the ending. Which one of her stuffed animals and dolls would Tabitha choose to act out the tale was part of the nightly drama.

He smiled as he exited the kitchen. Creativity was central to life just as love was the center of relationships and family. Was he ready to open his heart to more love and extending his poly family nucleus to embrace Jeff and Mary? He needed to connect with Mary more before he decided.

Jeff laid aside the latest action thriller novel he'd picked up in the hotel gift shop. He'd read the same three pages two nights in a row. It wasn't the author's fault he couldn't lose himself in the story. His thoughts were elsewhere. Mary mentioned talking with her shrink friend, Sharon, about him and Ron as they talked two nights ago. His stomach had flip-flopped during the entire conversation. Sweaty palms and worry had boiled and bubbled deep in the pit of his stomach.

He knew part of his reaction came from lack of sleep and long hours in the kitchen of Haute Cuisine. Things began running smoother with tonight's dinner rush. Susan and Tim had left smiling instead of bleary-eyed and yawning. Hiring the former hotel chef and an assistant took a few tries that none of them could have foreseen. Now, a talented cook with a high reputation ruled the kitchen and had taken the assistant chef under his wing. Jeff exhaled and leaned back against the pillows he propped himself up with.

Knowing that Mary was seeing Ron bothered him some and yet it didn't. He'd figured out poly was about knowing about the other loves and significant people in your loves life. He'd accepted Darcey and Lindsay's place in Mary's life. Even her clients that called outside of business hours because that was the way things ran when events happened. What made her and Ron being together different? Competition? Intentions? Some things nagged at him because he was tired and the unknowns added up to more unknowns. When did info overload stop, or was there such a thing?

He reached for the pad he'd listed his earlier thoughts on. The top item dealt with how much did he want to know. Number two raised the question of privacy and what did that entail. The list went on with bits and pieces of things that interconnected at various points. This must be the small stuff one blogger talked about. The things that become rules or guideposts changed as the relationships aged and morphed. This led him back to Mary's first question as they talked. Was he in and willing to give poly a shot? Probably yes with some reservations that needed discussion. He knew that for he and Mary to work out they needed one-on-one time. She needed the same with Ron. And there was the business venture they had briefly discussed before he left—hiring Darcey to oversee the party-planning side.

Jeff marked through two of the items on the list. They weren't realistic. No one could promise they wouldn't break up. They could work on avoiding it by keeping communication open and honest. Ona had mentioned that more than once during her weekly calls. She urged him to say what bothered him and what worked for him when he and Mary got together again with Ron. Owning his feelings was important if he wanted a long-term relationship. That might happen if his frazzled mind and subconscious would let him sleep without weird dreams. Maybe tonight was the night.

He put the book and pad on the nightstand. As he pulled the covers over him and pulled a pillow out from behind him, he blinked, yawned and blinked again. He turned the lamp off and closed his eyes. One last image flashed across his psyche as sleep claimed him—Mary smiling at both him and Ron, saying I love you. Was it possible?

Chapter Fifteen

A *Week Later*
    Ron glanced at his sister Abebi. Tabitha was zonked out on his couch. He cleared his throat. "Thanks for keeping an eye on things at the diner."

Abebi smiled, saying, "You're welcome. I can see now why you hired more help."

"Your idea of hiring students from the vocation school saved me a lot of time and money." Ron stood, picked up the comforter from the back of the chair close to him, and covered up Tabitha.

"My principal had an overwhelming response. The kids in the program love the opportunity you're giving them—a paycheck and work experience."

"Giving back to the community is important. Nana Rose and Mom taught us that." Ron stretched. "I'm hungry. Come on out to the kitchen. I'll fix us something."

"Thanks. A snack sounds good." Abebi checked on Tabitha and followed him into the kitchen. "She played hard and swam a lot. Darcey came up with a great idea of a picnic and pool party for Lindsay's fourth birthday."

"Darcey's quite the party planner. She's planned and executed on a few of the parties in San Francisco and Berkeley for Mary and me. I want to talk to Mary and Jeff about hiring Darcey." Ron put the loaf of bread and slices of cheese he got out of the fridge on the counter. "Split a grilled cheese sandwich?"

"Sounds good." Abebi got plates out of the cabinet and put them on the table. "Better make Tabitha one. She'll wake up when she smells the food."

Ron chuckled. "Yes, like her uncle. A foodie at heart."

He prepped the sandwich and laid it on the griddle, heating on top of the stove. "About five to ten minutes until our sandwich is done. I'll make Tabitha's when she wakes up."

"Okay. How about some chips to go with the sandwich?" Abebi set glasses filled with water on the table next to their plates.

"On top of the fridge." Ron turned the sandwich and faced Abebi. "I'm glad Nana Rose has her friends around her. I'm worried though."

"Why?"Abebi asked.

"She and her posse are starting a strip poker tournament Saturday nights at their duplex. Mixed couples strip poker!" Ron laughed and took the griddle off the stove. He put half of the sandwich on each of their plates.

"Maybe they're chaperoning each other." Abebi sat down as he ran water on the griddle.

"Nana Rose is something else. Feisty and talking about how women her age need safer sex talks, too." Ron sat down. "Eat while it's warm. I used Gouda and Muenster cheese slices."

"Oooh, the good stuff," Abebi said. She saluted him with her half and started eating. Several moments passed as they ate. As Abebi wiped her mouth, she pointed at him. "Nana Rose misses Grandpa Jack. Neither missed a chance to touch, hug, or kiss the other. Sensuality oozed off them."

Ron chuckled. "Yeah, Mom used to mutter about them getting a room."

Abebi picked up the last chip on her plate. "Yes, she did. She always smiled when she said it. Love like Nana Rose's and Grandpa Jack's doesn't happen for everyone."

"True. I hope you find the same with someone, sis." Ron stood.

Abebi pushed back from the table, stood up, and made her way to him. She threw her arms around him, hugging him tight. "I want the same for you, bro."

"Thanks, Abebi," Ron said, stepping back. "I think I hear Tabitha moving."

"I'll check on her." Abebi kissed his cheek and walked into the living room.

Ron put their dishes in the dishwasher and reached for the griddle when Abebi returned carrying Tabitha. "Thanks for offering to make her a sandwich, but she wants chicken tenders and mashed potatoes. We're off to Chicken Little."

Ron followed them back into the living room. "Okay. Let me know you got home safely."

"You bet," Abebi said, putting her purse and tote over her other shoulder. "I'll text you as soon as I get in."

He opened the front door and followed Abebi onto the porch.

Tabitha yawned, waved, and laid her head on her mother's shoulder. "Bye-bye Uncle Ron."

"Bye munchkin. Love you." He kissed Tabitha on the forehead.

"Love you, too," Tabitha sleepily responded.

He waited on his front porch until Abebi pulled away before he went back inside. Two things stuck in his thoughts as he cleaned up the kitchen. Neither he nor Abebi had found the partner that got them juicy in the way their grandparents had gotten each other. Maybe that was because conventionality didn't fit them. The few men Abebi had dated weren't interested in taking on a readymade family. As for him, he'd wanted kids and a wife in his twenties. No one he met was ready to settle down or work together toward a future they built in tandem. Like Jeff, it took him several years to figure out what he wanted and where. Culinary school offered more answers and opportunities for him than other jobs had. At forty, what did he want?

Ron filled the electric kettle with water, inserted the tea strainer full of loose leaf decaf orange blossom cinnamon tea, and put it on to boil. He set a mug on the counter and glanced at the wall clock hanging over the kitchen window. 5:45 p.m. He picked up his cell phone and dialed. Mary picked up on the third ring.

"Hey handsome," Mary said.

"Well, good looking ain't a curse," he bantered back.

"Never is in my book. How can I do you?" Mary asked.

"You really want to know?" he probed as the electric kettle started to whistle. He rose, cradling his phone to his ear with his shoulder. He turned the kettle off and filled his mug.

"Did I hear the teakettle?"

"Sure did. Orange Blossom Cinnamon. Why?"

Mary's *hmmmm* hummed through the phone. "Could use a cup and a snack. I'm two blocks away since my regular route home is backed up due to road work."

"Come on darlin'. We'll discuss in person how you can do me." Ron reached down and adjusted his fly. Hard-ons didn't get zippers and ball room when they raged on and sent his balls to swelling.

"Be right there, handsome," Mary responded and hung up.

Ron stood up, pocketed his cell phone, and put the kettle on to reheat. He placed another mug and a plate of homemade strawberry shortbread cookies on the table. Glancing at the clock again, he calculated how long until Mary arrived. Depending on which way she came from, the entrance to his subdivision could be two easy right turns or two long light left turns against oncoming traffic. Either way put her at his door within five to ten minutes. He trotted out of the kitchen, across the living room, and up the stairs to his bedroom.

He stuffed his dirty clothes into the hamper, closed the lid, and entered the bathroom. His towel hung over the shower curtain rod where he'd flung it in his hurry to shower and dress that morning. He pulled the towel off the rod and hung it on the towel rack. Another quick glance showed nothing else needed tidying in the bathroom or bedroom. He fluffed the pillows and straightened the sheets and hand-made quilt. Most of the time, he lived alone. Abebi helped with housekeeping while staying with him on her double shift weekends. At least he wasn't a total inept bachelor. He knew to sort lights and darks before washing them.

He kicked his deck shoes into the closet. As he closed the door, the doorbell rang. He smiled as he straightened. Mary had beaten the left turn lights. It was seven minutes since he talked with her.

"Be there in a moment," he called out, making his way down the last steps. As he reached the door, the electric kettle started whistling. He quickly opened the door. Mary stood on his front porch, her hand on her hips, winking at him.

"I hear there's snacks and tea here," Mary said, entering the living room.

Ron laughed and closed the front door. "Sure is. Maybe a few other things, too."

Mary placed her purse on the coffee table, reached down and slipped her sandals off before turning and facing him. "Dare I ask what those might be?"

Ron shoved his hands in his pockets, shrugged, and replied. "I'd say I don't tell and kiss. But kiss and tell..."

Mary moved tight to him, leaving little space between them as her feet touched his. "Oh, kiss away, handsome. And when done, do tell."

Ron glanced down, noting where his and Mary's feet were. He straddled hers and moved closer leaving no space between them from the waist down. He took his hands out of his pockets, looped his arms around Mary's neck, and pressed more fully against her.

Mary's sudden inhale thrust her breasts against him, leaving no doubt of his effect on her. He'd gotten to her for sure. Her taut nipples brushed against him each breath she took. When she exhaled and rocked back a bit, her mons rubbed him and his hard cock.

"I think you're more than ready for this kiss," he said, tilting his head slightly to the right. He threaded his fingers into Mary's hair, cradling her head with the palm of his hand. Her gaze met his. She nodded briefly, tilted her head opposite his, and placed her lips on his. He parted his lips and met the tip of her tongue with his.

Mary closed her eyes as Ron's lips parted beneath hers. He met her partway into her foray tasting him. His woodsy aftershave greeted her each breath she took. Hints of juniper, balsam, and ginger punctuated the tastes of orange and cinnamon she got each time his tongue touched hers. Sips taunted her, calling her to come in and taste every inch of his delicious mouth. Dare she press forward and take the lead? Ron hadn't declared his dominance or preference in leading their prior makeout sessions. At some point, either of them had led. She hadn't asked Ron outright if he was egalitarian in views. Their discussions centered on politics, current affairs and community events. At no point had Ron come across as a staunch believer of one set of strict ideals. He listened to both sides and offered his opinion. His opinion right now was to kiss her senseless. He followed her retreat with his tongue, tasting and drinking her passion as thoroughly as she had him.

She pulled back, breaking off the French kiss. Inhaling, she opened her eyes and found him watching her. His hand cradled her head while his other palm lay warm in the small of her back, steadying her against him. He rubbed his thumb up and down over a spot she hadn't let on about. A narrow portion between her waist and hips that tingled, sending bursts of searing pleasure up and down her back. Jeff found out about the sweet spot massaging her back one evening after a long, busy day at the shop. Now Ron had found it on his own. Her nipples pulsed every time he stroked upward on her back. If she gave in and arched her shoulders, straightening her back, she'd pull away from the wonderful hard cock pushing against her.

"Think you're ready to hear the tell part?" Ron whispered hotly into her ear. He caught her earlobe between his teeth, worrying it as his fingers plucked and gently tweaked her swollen nipples.

"I-I think so," she responded, arching her shoulders and pressing her mons tighter to Ron.

Ron let go of her earlobe, laved it twice before nibbling his way down her neck to her shoulder as he lightly pinched and pulled her nipples. He slid his hand down her hip until he cupped one cheek of her ass. He squeezed and patted her ass and dropped his hand, moving a step back until cool air wafted up amid them. Mary swallowed, licked her lips, and said, "You gonna leave me wondering or..." She let her voice trail off.

Ron chuckled, rested his forehead against hers, and replied, "Oh, no wondering needed, darlin'. I want to make you squirm until you beg me to stop. That would take several days." Ron pulled back again, smirking and winking.

"I-I don't think I'd last that long." Damn, why did she keep stammering?

He grinned and shrugged. "How about I take a couple of hours tasting you? Then stroke both of us to more delightful orgasms."

She blinked and swallowed. Her retort died before she even spoke. Instead, she winked and said, "I'm game if you are."

Ron turned from her and started toward the kitchen where the kettle kept whistling. "Well, we could just have tea and cookies."

"Sustenance after a vigorous sex session is always refreshing." Mary made her way to the stairs and faced Ron, who'd stopped at the kitchen doorway. "Unless you've started keeping condoms in the fridge."

Ron turned toward her, chuckling and shaking his head. "Abebi finally convinced Tabitha my bedroom and bathroom were off-limits. Keeping certain things under lock and key from an inquisitive four-and-a-half-year-old is difficult."

Mary chortled. "Lindsay's been asking Jeff questions like she's the local D.A. investigating him."

Ron nodded. "Four years old and think they know the world. Come into the kitchen for a moment, please." Had Mary and Jeff moved forward on having sex? The last he'd talked to her they were still hashing out things.

He glanced over his shoulder as he entered the kitchen. Mary followed with a puzzled look on her face. He turned the kettle off and picked it up, moving to the sink as he spoke. "Are you and Jeff having sex? Figured things out?"

Mary leaned against the chair closest to her. "Those are loaded questions."

"True. Things that I've learned to ask from past relationships. If part of the couple or people you're seeing are having issues, they become yours." Ron pulled the tea strainer out of the kettle and set it in the sink.

"I get what you're talking about. It's like when Susan, Jeff, and I were in business together. If any two of us had issues, the third had 'em, too, like it or not."

"It's not quite that stressful unless you over-invest in the relationship without talking things out." Ron poured the tea into a pitcher and put it in the fridge. He ran water in the kettle and set it in the sink. "What is up with you and Jeff?"

Mary held up four fingers. "One, he knows I'm here with you." She put one finger down.

"Okay."

"Two, we're talking about what we want and how that relates to the three of us."

"Good. You'll share what you can."

"Three, I don't know if quickies count. We've done those and spent a couple of nights together."

Ron laughed. "Depends on your quickie definitions. Did you practice safe sex?"

Mary nodded. "Four, safe sex practiced for sure. Ruined more friggin' condoms trying to rip the packet open than we actually used."

Ron pressed his lips together lest he burst out laughing. He inhaled, looked away and back at Mary. "How many did you use?"

Mary held up one finger. "Lindsay kept knocking on the door wanting to know what Jeff was doing in my room. Seems she's laid claim to him and calls him her poopyhead."

"Oh lord," Ron said in between outbursts of laughter. "Sounds like Jeff is getting family acceptance."

Mary chuckled. "Oh yeah. He told me that if he could pass Lindsay's standards, he must not be such a bad fellow."

Ron pulled Mary into his arms and hugged her tight. "We'll practice opening those condom packets so you can do better next time and forgo only doing quickies. Sound good?"

"Sure, if you can remember where you put the key to that lock you talked about." Mary slipped out of his embrace, entwining one hand with his as she did.

"Well, let's go upstairs and I'll show you my hiding place." Ron exited the kitchen still holding Mary's hand.

Chapter Sixteen

Ron paused at his bedroom door. Mary hadn't gotten this far the first time they made out like a couple of lusty, hormone-driven teens. His clothes and hers had littered the front room and coffee table. After dinner, drinks had turned into mutual masturbation and nude cuddles. That had been three months into Jeff's Europe sojourn. The night Jeff called and said he'd be staying longer.

Mary squeezed his hand. "I'm ready if you are."

Ron smiled, leaned down, and brushed his lips over hers. "We've come close a couple of times. And backed off each time. I'm making sure we're both ready this time."

Mary raised his hand, kissed each knuckle, and rubbed her cheek against them. "I told Jeff that I wanted to move forward with your and my part of the relationship. This also includes sex."

Ron moved into the bedroom. He sat down on his bed, patting the space next to him. "Sit down. I want to get a few things out of the way before we go further."

Mary sat down and started to scoot away from him. He laid a hand on her arm. "Hey, it's okay. I do this with every relationship. I like to start out on the same page."

"Okay." Mary moved back until a few inches separated them.

He smiled and reached for her hand. "I tend to be egalitarian on many things. One thing I strongly believe in is no means no. The same with stop."

"Thank you for reassuring me. Some men don't get that. You and Jeff do."

Ron let go of Mary's hand, slipped his arm around her shoulders, and continued speaking. "I can fuck if that's what you want. I can make love, too. Be passionate and playful. I prefer to be a lover."

Mary leaned into him, smiling. "The L word is getting a lot of use."

"What do you mean?" he asked, leaning back on his hands.

"Jeff and I figured out we'd fallen in love a few months before he left. Neither of us realized it until we talked about our relationship recently." Mary stretched out beside him.

"So where does that leave us?" Ron lay on his side facing Mary.

"I prefer lovers. I've fallen for you or I wouldn't be here."

"Are you saying you love me?" Ron laid his hand on Mary's waist.

"Not sure. I know I care a lot. Loving someone is risky."

"Agreed. I get where you're coming from. Are you ready to move into lovers and friends with me?"

Mary moved across the bed over until she lay very close to him. "Lovers and friends sounds wonderful."

"Good, 'cuz I love to pleasure my lovers. And I'm going to make you purr, darlin." Ron slid an arm around Mary and brushed his lips over hers. "First step is to get rid of some of these clothes."

Mary stood up. Pulled her t-shirt over her head, tossed it on the bed, and reached for the waistband of her shorts. She glanced at Ron, who watched her intently.

"Keep going. I like the view." Ron propped his head up with one hand, leaning on his elbow. A soft thud followed.

She looked down at the floor. Ron's flip-flops lay crisscrossed on the rug. "Good, you've started stripping I see."

"Yup. Your turn. I took an item off." Ron sat up, pulling his polo shirt over his head. "I'm one up on you. You gotta take two off now."

Mary grinned. "Well, that will leave me near-nude."

"Not a bad option if you ask me." Ron tossed his shirt on the bed. It landed near her top. He stood, undoing his belt and fly button. "I can even things up if you like."

Mary shrugged and shucked her shorts. "Take your jeans off. Even-steven works for me."

Ron chuckled. "I'm glad we're past the awkward stage of things."

"Awkward how?" Mary asked, sitting down on the bed.

Ron shucked his jeans as he answered her. "Getting undressed in front of each other."

He tossed his jeans on the bed close to their tops. He turned around, bent over, and twerked at her. Then stood up, faced her, and said, "Now do we strip or make out more?"

Mary burst out laughing. Continued laughing each time she looked at Ron, who started laughing, too. He sat beside her as their sustained mutual laughter lasted several moments longer. Mary wiped her eyes as she spoke. "Oh gosh, that was good. That's another reason why I enjoy spending time with you. Joy and laughter."

"Thank you," Ron said, slipping an arm around her shoulders. "I like those things in my partners, too. Thanks for having them."

Mary turned, looping her arms around Ron's neck. "I think stripping and making out tied."

Ron nodded, leaned close to her, and whispered, "Correct answer, and the lady wins lots more kisses."

Mary tilted her head back until she could see Ron clearly. "Ah, do we need to find your hiding place first?"

Ron snorted, kissed her forehead, and pulled away. "Medicine chest top shelf. Out of sight, out of mind of an inquisitive four-year-old's line of sight."

"Took a bit to teach Lindsay about asking for help reaching things. They're so independent." Mary scooted to the end of the bed and stood. She reached between her breasts and undid the center clasp of her bra. "Strip first or get condoms first?"

Ron rose, took hold of the waistband of his briefs, and pulled them down until his hips were bare. He didn't need to look down to know part of his pelvic hair showed. The other thing that stopped him was his hard cock. He ached and needed to come. How much longer could he hold out?

"Strip, darlin', strip. I'm going for the condoms." Ron shoved his briefs down over his cock and legs. He stepped out of them, kicking them aside as he started toward the bathroom. "By the way, aqua becomes you."

He blew a kiss at Mary as he reached the bathroom door. She hadn't moved or spoke since he told her to strip. He glanced at Mary, blew her another kiss, and trotted into the bathroom. She'd started slipping her bra straps down her arms. Good. Every time she bantered back and took off another piece of clothing, he got closer to pleasuring them both. Action he was looking forward to. He grabbed the box of condoms and turned around. He stiffened, rocking forward on his toes.

Mary stood inside the bathroom door, nude. She worked her hair into a loose ponytail and strode toward the shower. "I like a clean cock and balls to kiss and fondle. What about you?" She opened the shower door, turned the water on and faced him.

Ron set the condom box on the counter, pulled his towel and another off the towel rack, and laid them on the counter. "Oh, I love a clean and sweet-tasting clit."

Mary gave him a come-hither motion with her fingers, stepped into the shower and closed the door. Ron spun around, plucked two washcloths off the stack he kept on the counter near the sink, and walked to the shower. He slid the door open at the opposite end and stepped in behind Mary.

Water splashed off Mary and onto him. He reached behind her, grasping the bottle of shower gel, holding it out to her as he wet his washcloth. "Been a while since I got a good back scrub. Do you mind?" He turned around, offering Mary his wet washcloth. "A bit of shower gel works up a good lather."

"Sure," Mary answered. "You gotta do mine, too."

Ron chortled. "You bet! Right along with helping you wash the rest of you."

A warm, wet stroke started at his left shoulder, dipped partway down his back and up to his right shoulder. Others mixed with side-to-side ones started across his upper back. He arched his shoulders and started to turn.

"Hold on," Mary scolded. "Got two more places to get."

"Huh?" Ron tried to look over his shoulder. He blinked as water splashed on his face. Two swift wipes crossed one ass cheek and then his other.

Mary's soft tittered sounded. "Okay, done with this side. Turn around."

Ron slowly turned until he faced Mary, whose smile lit up her face like a kid with a secret they were dying to tell. "Pleased with your efforts?" he asked.

"Mostly. Gotta finish the job." Mary laid her washcloth-covered hand on his chest and rubbed in a circular motion until she spread the lather over him. She next stroked over his stomach and lower toward his cock and balls. She looked up as she took hold of him.

"Ah, yes. Been waiting for you to touch me there." Ron ducked his head, his eyes closing. "Your hands feel great on me."

"Good," Mary replied, working the soapy cloth up and down his cock and over his balls. "I remember your touch like it was yesterday. I'm glad we decided to keep on seeing each other."

Ron reached for the soapy washcloth Mary held. "Enough or I'm going to come now. It'll take me time to recover."

"I'd rather you come inside me," Mary countered, handing Ron the cloth. "Need more gel?"

"Couldn't hurt. Turn around after you hand it to me." Ron took the shower gel from her. He added another dollop to the cloth and handed her the bottle.

Mary took the bottle, turned around, and leaned over to replace it back on the corner of the tub. Ron worked the washcloth over her shoulders and back. She turned around. "We gonna keep talking and soaping or you gonna get on with the necessary parts?"

Ron grinned. "Oh, there's plenty of time. Delaying the titillating part of pleasure peaks it, too."

"Pffftt is my response." She reached for the washcloth, determined to wash her breasts and mons herself.

"No, you can't have it." Ron held the cloth away from her. "I'm washing these." He tweaked her nipple, rolling it between his thumb and finger, pulling it slightly as he did.

"Hmmm. That is good." Mary arched her neck, rolled her shoulders, and tried to inhale.

"Behave and you might get more," Ron whispered as he leaned closer. "Now arms up and let the washing commence."

Mary raised her arms, replying, "I'm *good at everything* I do."

Ron looked away, caught the inside of his bottom lip between his teeth and looked back. Mary stood in front of him with her arms raised, winking and grinning cheekily. He worked the soapy washcloth up and down the arm closest to him, trailed it across the top of her chest and up and down her other arm. Stepping closer to Mary, he slid one palm under her breast, holding it as he ran the cloth over her, getting close to her areola and nipple but not touching them. He lifted her breast higher, capturing her nipple with his lips. He nipped and suckled, drawing her rigid nipple as deep as he could into the heat of his mouth. He licked the tip twice and let go. He paid similar homage to her other breast and nipple.

Ron moved back and washed Mary's stomach and hips. Wringing the cloth between his hands, he said, "Lower your arms. You're good at some things, I see."

He waited until she lowered her arms before adding, "Spread your legs, darlin'. Time to wash your lovely clit."

Mary spread her legs as far as she could. Ron combed his soapy fingers down through the thatch of hair covering her mons. He inserted one finger, then another. Stroking backward until he found what he sought.

"Can't take much. Very sensitive." Mary shuddered, reaching for him. She laid one hand on his shoulder. Her other hand gripped his upper arm as he sped up his strokes.

"Just a small come. I want to feel and see your pleasure. It turns me on." He stroked back and forth faster than his last. Over and around her clit until Mary groaned deeply.

Ron dropped the cloth, slipped his arms around Mary's waist, and hugged her. He could feel every breath she took. The rise and fall of her chest and breasts touched him. Flesh-to-flesh, they stood until he felt her take a deep breath several moments later. Mary looked up, blinked, and tried to smile.

He brushed his lips over hers. "Nice beginning."

"Yeah. I agree." Mary inhaled again and tried to straighten up.

"Are you sure that's a good idea?" Ron asked, keeping an arm tight around Mary's waist.

"Yes. Got to wash you." Mary took hold of his cock and stroked down him, squeezing lightly until she reached his balls. She slid her hand lower, cupping them.

Ron rocked his hips back and forth, working his cock in and out of the circle of Mary's fingers. Her next stroke upward didn't stop until she reached his glans. Sensitive and wet with pre-come, he shuddered and jerked as Mary's fingers glided over him, dampening her hand and him with his wetness.

"Easy. I'm like your clit. Want to taste me or have me on your hand?" He stepped back, placing a hand on Mary's shoulder as he leaned down. If she kept up the light squeezing strokes, he didn't think he could hold back. Hell, after they got out of the shower, he hoped she didn't mind a quickie cuz that was about how long he'd last. Long enough to pull a condom on and work his way inside her. How many strokes he'd have until he came, he didn't know. Could he bring her off again between playing with her and thrusting in and out at the same time?

Ron handed Mary the soapy washcloth. "Easy, light strokes. Then we're out of here."

Mary nodded, slowly working the cloth over his cock and balls. "Excited works both ways. I want you, too. Passion peaks then..."

She handed him the soapy cloth and stepped around him, ducking under the spray. Mary exited the shower, leaving him standing there holding a soapy washcloth, wondering if she was hinting at something.

"Uhmm," he called out. "You going somewhere?"

Ron ducked under the spray, rinsing him and the washcloth. He wrung the cloth out, tossing it on the rack in the back of the shower.

"Depends on what you call somewhere," Mary bantered. "I'm drying off so I can get wetter in other places very soon."

Ron grabbed his towel, drying off rapidly. "Oh darlin', that is a sure thing."

Mary laughed and grabbed opposite ends of the towel in each hand, twirling them until the towel wrapped around itself. She turned sideways, pulling the towel back, grinning.

"Don't do it," Ron chided, hanging his towel up. "I'll make you beg for the first orgasm."

Mary nodded, answering, "Yes. You did that the first time. Maybe paybacks are due."

"Oh, you think so?" Ron challenged, moving toward her with his hand out.

"I wonder how long you can hold out," Mary razzed, letting go of one end of her towel.

Ron chuckled, taking hold of her towel. He pulled it taut between them, leaned back, and tugged hard. "How about we don't worry about that and work on mutual orgasms instead?"

Mary rocked back, bent her knees, and let the towel slide through her hands some. She smiled, winked, and moved forward until inches separated them. "Mutual is divine. You think you're up to the task?"

"You'll have to find out, won't you?" Ron let go of the towel and sauntered out of the bathroom.

Mary shoved her towel onto the towel rack next to Ron's and trotted into the bedroom.

Chapter Seventeen

R on patted the space next to him. "Condoms ready. I'm ready. Ride or taste?"

Mary gulped. Tasting and riding—her two favorite forms of sexual play. She had missed Jeff's saltiness with a touch of sweet taste while he was gone. Her only taste of Ron reminded her of almond butter with that bit of tang and smoothness mixed with a hint of salt.

"A loss for words? Well, I didn't expect this," Ron said, cupping his balls with one hand and his cock with his other.

Mary shook her head, kneeling on the bed. "No loss for words. Deciding where to put my tongue first."

Ron glanced at her. His eyes were partly closed. She knew that look. Need coursed through him. Enveloping him from the tip of his cock all the way down to his balls and even tightening his insides into an *I-need-to-come knot*, she bet.

Ron nodded. "Okay, you drive."

Mary stayed on her hands and knees, looking up and down Ron. "Sixty-nine."

"You sure?" Ron rose on his elbows, looking at Mary still on her hands and knees.

"Honey," Mary began, straddling him. "I can hold a yoga plank with the best of them. Lay back and let the taste test begin."

He chuckled, resumed lying on his back, and waited. Mary slowly turned around until her breath grazed his cock as she lowered her head.

He licked his finger, reaching up with his other hand. Her swollen clit stood out, glistening with its pre-come coating. He was about to find out if his memories were true.

Over and around, he traced her clit with the pad of his finger. Mary's muffled hums of pleasure reached him. She jerked toward him each time he brushed the top of her clit twice. He glanced up, noting the wetness pooling outside of her vagina. One more stroke and he slid his finger into her, thrusting it in and out like he would as she rode him.

"Oh man," he groaned as Mary's fingers wrapped around him and started stroking. "You are keeping me hot."

He stuck out his tongue, puckered, and started licking. He captured her clit between his lips, increasing the pace of each lap.

"Want to taste you," Mary rapidly said. "I-I am..."

She didn't finish. She couldn't. Her eyes closed as shivers and shudders engulfed her. Bursts of colors, flashes of light, and a kaleidoscope of images rushed across her mind. Her clit tightened, pulsed, and the first wave of orgasm swamped her. Back and forth she rocked as the next wave rippled from her nipples, over her breast, down through her, and deep into her swollen tingling clit. She forced her eyes open, pulling away from Ron. "Please stop. More and I am done."

Ron stopped. "You okay?" He rubbed his hands up and down her back and hips.

Mary inhaled, held her breath, and exhaled. "Yes. I want to taste you before we try mutual orgasm."

Ron rested his hands on her back. "Making sure. I'm fine with going for the mutual without a BJ."

Mary rolled onto her side as she moved off Ron. "Relax. Going take a taste before I put a condom on you."

Ron nodded. "Go for it." He tucked his hands behind his head and spread his legs.

She rolled over, picked up a condom packet, and tore it open. Rising to a sitting position, Mary faced Ron, holding the packet where he could see it. "I'm going to taste and cover you. Okay?"

Ron nodded. He smiled, blew her a kiss, and nodded again.

Mary pressed her lips together to control her mirth. She grinned, blew Ron a kiss back, and rose onto her knees. She faced toward the foot of the bed, working the condom out of the packet. Not tearing the first one or ruining it like she and Jeff had in their haste to couple a few days earlier, she eased the condom out of the foil onto the palm of her hand. Keeping the condom in one fist while she scooted across the bed took some maneuvering. Scoot, slide, scoot, slide got her where she wanted, touching Ron's leg close to his groin.

Ron stuffed one of the pillows more under his head and neck. He wanted to watch Mary enjoy herself while pleasuring him. Seeing a woman enjoy intimacy fueled his own pleasure. It deepened his to a point he came longer and harder when the energy and chemistry blended well.

"Oh yes," he groaned. Her cool hand touching him sent not one but two jolts deep into his groin. Hitting him right where he boiled, his balls. Shivers followed by growing waves of need boiled upward, ready to steam out of his lower half, scalding its way up to his mind, the other sexiest part of him.

Mary brushed her lips over and across his glans dampening him.

"Salty, just like I remember," Mary quickly replied.

"I-I'm gla—" The rest of his reply died in his throat because of where Mary's lips were, puckered around his cockhead with her tongue flicking back and forth over it. Ron lowered his hips to the bed. He bunched balls of sheet and blankets against his palms as he fisted and clenched his hands as Mary slowly, inch by exposed inch of him, deep throating him. She reached down and started fondling his balls.

"Mu-much more and there won't be more," he managed to get out as Mary started a slow upward pull of her lips.

Mary let go of him and nodded. Air brushed over him, sending shivers and quivers down over his balls. He was wet. She'd managed to lubricate him naturally while reminding each of them what their first time was like.

Mary took ahold of Ron near the base of his cock, cupped his glans with her other palm, holding the condom and eased it down over him until both hands held him close to his balls. Releasing one hand, then her other, she surveyed her handiwork. The condom fit him closely from midway down his glans to near the base of his balls. The reservoir tip showed plenty of room. She leaned forward, placing both hands on the bed, and turned until she faced Ron.

She looked up, noting how tightly fisted his hands were. "You okay?" she asked, catching his gaze.

"Oh yeah," he said, followed by a short, breathy sigh. "Need to come soon or gonna lose it."

"Got ya," she said, swinging one leg over Ron. She rocked left and right until she comfortably straddled him. Mary worked her way backward down Ron until his cock came into view. She looked up, catching him watching her. "Ready?"

She took hold of him as she scooted backward a bit more. He nodded, taking a deep breath and exhaling. She rose on her knees, rocked forward, and slowly guided Ron into her.

Full penetration. Their first time. Every man felt different and yet there was a sameness to it. The fullness that came with joining together in a very age-old dance. She tightened her muscles, squeezing and flexing, getting used to his fit and the places he touched, like a good portion of her G-spot. She relaxed, inhaling and watching Ron's reaction.

"Just like I imagined. It's great to be inside you." Ron rocked back and forth beneath her, thrusting in and out in a slow rhythm.

"You feel great, too. I love the way you rub my G-spot." Mary tried to counter her up and down motion counter to Ron's. It didn't work. He kept rubbing and reaching the tender parts of her G-spot and vagina. She inhaled, sank down on her knees, taking all of Ron inside her until their pubic hairs meshed together.

Ron reached between him and Mary. Running his thumb along the crease of her labia, he coated his thumb pad with some of her wetness. Carefully, he reached inside, stroking and caressing until he found her clit. Pulsing and engorged, it greeted him, begging for a stroke, a touch, and pressure taunting it until its interior cousin relaxed its grip on their shared muscles.

Mary tightened around him as he sped up his strokes. He lowered his hips to the bed, saying, "Take control, darlin'. We're both ready to orgasm."

Mary's breaths shortened. He watched her nipples tighten more and her eyes close. She leaned forward, balancing on her hands laying on him close to his hips. She started riding him in short, uneven bounces. He picked up speed and strokes over and across her clit. Two strokes—and she went rigid. Her eyes were fully closed, he caught as she tossed her head back. She tightened around him, gasped, and let out a low moan that seemed to come from deep inside her. She started shaking as he kept rubbing her clit. Another strong pulse gripped him as another round of multiple orgasms hit her.

Bright lights filled his eyes as his balls pulled tight to him, hot and heavy, pounding with need. He rocked his hips forward and back, ready to lift them off the bed when it hit him. Colors, vibrant colors, replaced the bright lights. Reds, greens, and yellows burst forth like fireworks on a hot Fourth of July night. They erupted and faded to return with each spurt of jisim he shot. All the way from the bottom of his balls up out of his cock, the waves of orgasms grabbed him, tossed him on the wave of another pulse from Mary, egging him on to shoot another shot of semen into the condom and all over himself.

Moments passed. Neither of them spoke. Mary lay across him where he helped her to after she fell forward on their last mini-mutual orgasm. He didn't want to move, open his eyes, or speak. Breathing was all he could manage. Some people said when sex got this good, love was part of the mix. He didn't know if that was it or their wait grew the anticipation of this moment. Whatever it was, he wanted to repeat it again and again.

Ron cracked one eye open as Mary entwined her fingers with his. He blinked and opened both eyes. Her gaze met his. She smiled and blew him a kiss. He raised his head and brushed his lips over hers. Lying back, he said, "Wow!"

Mary echoed his feelings. "Wow for sure."

"Could use a short nap," Mary murmured.

Ron slid to the edge of the bed and stood up. "Crawl under the blankets. I need to use the bathroom. I'll be right back."

Mary pulled part of the blanket over her as he entered the bathroom. He discarded the condom in the trash, washed his hands and ran a damp washcloth over him. He didn't bother looking in the mirror. No one looked like they stepped out of a fashion magazine layout after making love. There was that word again. L-O-V-E, the one item that his heart whispered while his mind said nah. He yawned and exited the bathroom.

Mary lay on her side facing him. She flung the blanket back, got up, and hurried past him. Noises similar to his followed. He grinned, shook his head, and crawled into bed. Straightening the sheet and blanket, he turned on his side so Mary could get in beside him and spoon until they drifted off.

"I promise I don't snore," Mary said, getting under the covers.

"Don't worry about it if you do. I'm prone to it some." Ron curled his body around Mary. "Don't think we'll sleep long. Awesome orgasms and naps go together."

Mary cuddled up to him, resting her head on his shoulder with a pillow beneath her head. He felt her breathing slow and deepen as his did. Two thoughts claimed his last cognizant thoughts—he'd been looking for love and maybe it found him.

Chapter Eighteen

T*wo hours later*
Ron handed Mary a rewarmed cup of chamomile tea and a plate of spaghetti and meatballs. "Sorry for the canned sauce. Best I could do on short notice. Tomorrow is grocery shopping night."

Mary set the mug on the table next to the plate of steaming food. "Look, we do what we can with what we got. I got us garlic bread thanks to the garlic powder you have and the half stick of butter I found on the fridge door."

"Yes. Quick meatballs with the crusts off the loaf of bread and an egg mixed with the tail end of the chub of hamburger I had stashed back for SOS gravy worked out," Ron agreed, laying napkins and utensils on the table.

"A homemade meal shared with someone you care about enriches what you got to eat." Mary picked up her mug, holding it out. "Here's to a fine dinner."

Ron touched his mug to Mary's. He looked at his watch as he picked up his fork. "Twelve minutes until the cookies are done. Sugar cookies a la mode with Belgian double chocolate chip ice cream ups this to fine dining, if you ask me."

Mary laughed, set her mug down, and started eating.

Several minutes passed before either of them looked up from their plates. Ron wiped his mouth and leaned back in his chair. "More than I can finish tonight. I got leftovers for tomorrow."

Mary pointed to her near-empty plate. "Sorry, not much left here. Maybe a piece or two of garlic bread." She pointed to the plate sitting between them.

"Don't sweat it. I enjoy people enjoying their meals. Eating is sensual if you're willing to acknowledge it."

Mary snorted as she picked up her mug. "Good thing I hadn't drank any tea yet. You are either a foodie at heart or a connoisseur of innuendos."

"Or a connoisseur of your tasty bits along with fine dining." Ron drank most of his tea, watching Mary fight off blushing.

She peered at him over the top of the mug as she sipped. She looked away, reached down, tugged at her top, and sipped more tea. Ron continued drinking the rest of his tea. He set his mug down on the table when the timer rang in the kitchen. He rose, picking up his plate and utensils. "Honey, it's wonderful you still blush." He wet a finger and drew a line down, awarding himself a point.

"You are bad," Mary said, shaking a finger at him as he walked by.

"Nah, just know what I want and what I like," he called out from the kitchen. "Would you please bring your plate in here?"

Mary gathered the rest of the dinner items from the table and carried them into the kitchen. She plugged the sink, started running hot water, and added dish detergent. She turned, leaning against the counter as she spoke. "You dropping hints or is that start of another conversation?"

"Both," Ron answered, taking the cookie sheet out of the oven. "Hint of what I want to talk about and beginning a discussion if you're game."

Mary got bowls from the cabinet along with the ice cream scoop. She took the ice cream out of the freezer as she answered. "I reserve my complete response until I know the topic. I'm open to talking more."

"Good. You finally told Jeff about the details of Warren's death and how you married him?"

"Yes, I did."

Ron put two cookies in each bowl and the rest on a cooling sheet. He set the pan on the counter and faced Mary. "Did you love Warren? I've never heard you say you did."

Mary swallowed hard. She hadn't admitted her misgivings even up through taking her vows. Neither Warren nor Darcey ever doubted her care and love over the years. She looked up and said, "At first, no. It took me a couple of years to grow into love with Warren. Why do you ask?"

"The few times I've said I care, even let the word love out, you've never said it back. Or said how you feel about us."

She shook out her hands and wiped her sweaty palms on her shorts. "Once I fell in love with Warren I never looked back. I threw myself into the loving mother and wife role."

"I got that from our talks. Also from what Abebi shared from her and Darcey's talks." Ron took two spoons out of the drawer. "Cookies are cool enough for the ice cream."

"Darcey talked about what?" Mary added a scoop of ice cream to each bowl. She rinsed the scoop and put it in the soapy water with the other dishes.

Ron took the pint of ice cream from her. "Take a breath. Darcey talked about missing her dad and mom. She said you came along when she and Warren needed someone."

Mary sighed. "I'm not sure what that means."

Ron put the ice cream in the freezer, walked back to the counter, picked up the bowls and headed back toward the dining room. "I don't think you have anything to worry about. I've never heard Darcey talk bad about you."

Mary sat down, toying with her napkin. "Sometimes you wonder if you did a good job as a parent. I look at Darcey and think, yeah. Sometimes I wonder if I'm taking too much credit."

Ron picked up his spoon, filled it with ice cream and a warm cookie, and saluted her. "Darcey got two moms who love and care about her. Watch her with Lindsay and the kids at the daycare. She is a great mom and a talented teacher."

Mary smiled, picked up her spoon, and dug into her dessert. "Thanks. Back to how I feel about us, you and me."

Ron nodded, eating more of his dessert.

"After Warren died, I hid, scared to think about other men, unsure how to feel or deal with much of anything except taking care of Darcey and going to work."

"I get it. I went through a lost phase myself after my divorce. Not sure who to trust, even me." Ron put his spoon in his bowl and pushed it away from him. He laid his hand palm up on the table. "Do you trust me?"

Mary looked down at Ron's hand, back at her bowl and hand holding her spoon, and at Ron. "Trust has multiple meanings. If you mean do I believe you, have faith in you and what you say, there is part of me that does."

"Okay. Can you explain that further?" Ron started to pull his hand back.

Mary leaned forward, laying her hand near Ron's. "I'm careful about who I trust. Before Warren, I got burned with relationships off and on. After him, well, I didn't know how to be vulnerable and protect me at the same time."

"Valid points. How do I make you feel?" Ron laid his other hand on hers.

Mary inhaled, closed her eyes, and focused on her heartbeat. Strong, steady, and—normal as Sharon would say each time she had her stop to check her pulse. "Warm, desired and cared about. You're a friend and a lover."

"I give a bit of my heart to those I'm intimate with. What about you?"

Mary pressed her lips together, looked away for several moments, and turned back. "I don't jump into bed with just anyone. I've got to feel good about them and the risky part of intimacy."

"So you give a piece of you, too, is what I think you're saying." Ron squeezed her hand. "That's good stuff." He lifted her hand to his mouth, kissing each knuckle until he turned her hand over, pressing one last kiss into the palm of her hand and closing her fingers into it.

Mary opened her mouth, closed it, and opened it again. She raised her closed hand to her mouth, pressed it against her lips as she nodded. She'd hoped, dreamed, and hoped again that she'd discover someone who'd understand her. A man who loved with his entire being. Loved with his heart, mind, and soul...a man who treasured relationships and got what it meant to be a collaborator as well as a leader if needed. She could stand strong on her own. Warren had made sure she could take care of herself. Still sometimes, it was nice to have someone step in and pick up where she left off. She wanted someone who didn't mind a cohort that took action with them, formed a partnership that could withstand good or bad times. Had she found him without knowing it? Found two men who walked into her heart, putting pieces of theirs in where they claimed a piece of hers?

Ron rose, walked around the table, and leaned down. He slipped an arm around her shoulders. "Blows you away when someone reads you without you having to explain, right?"

Mary nodded, leaning into Ron. "Scary and exhilarating at the same time. Unnerving, too."

"I understand." Ron hugged her and let go. He sat back down. "Velma and Ed got to me the same way."

"Velma and Ed?"

"I fell hard for Velma. She picked up on my needs without me having to say much." Ron leaned back in his chair. Mary put her hands on the table, palms down. Sweat slicked the table. Was he going to say there were others he felt the same way about?

"What happened?" Mary inhaled slowly, willing her heart to not cry out.

"I was new to poly and looking for love after a short, intense relationship that left me heartbroken." Ron picked up his napkin, tearing pieces off it. "I was ready to marry the girl that walked out on me."

"Ouch," Mary said. "Double ouch."

"At the time, yeah. Now, I understand where I fucked up." Ron tossed his napkin and the torn pieces on the table.

"Are you trying to tell me something?"

Ron smiled, snickered, and leaned forward. "Sharing what a dumbass I was then compared to now."

"How so?"

"I thought I was supposed to be the man. The big provider and shot caller. Boy, did I get that wrong!"

Mary pushed back from the table, brows arched, wide-eyed, and pointing at him, her mouth hanging open.

"Yeah me. The biggest jackass I knew next to a few other guys who brayed louder than me." Ron shook his head as he continued speaking. "Macho males weren't in high demand. Then I went soft, not knowing balance mattered."

"You, a submissive?" Mary looked away, her hand covering her mouth.

Ron chortled. "You can laugh out loud. I wasn't that meek and weak. I didn't know about being strong for myself."

"You found out somewhere."

"Right when Velma brought out the floggers and ropes, along with the blindfold. I got up and walked out."

Mary shook her head a couple of times and leaned back in her chair. Ron nodded, adding, "Velma handed them to Ed and said, 'looks like we found our new toy.'"

"I hope you ran."

"As fast as my feet would move." Ron rocked forward, holding up his hand. "After a few sessions with a life coach, I put two and two together."

"Strength comes from being you and taking care of yourself?"

"Similar. I learned about putting my heart out to everyone. I began exercising choice and checking in with me."

Mary licked her lips as her cell phone rang. Ron picked it up, glancing at the caller ID. "It's Jeff. You want to take this alone?"

"No. He knows I'm here." Mary took her phone. She pushed the talk button. "Hi, Jeff. What's up?"

"Got back about an hour ago. Wanted to see if you and Ron were open to me coming over."

"Let me check." Mary muted her phone, looking at Ron. "Jeff wants to come over. What do you think?"

Ron looked at his watch. "It's only seven-thirty. Why not?"

Mary shrugged. "I can't think of any. I hope he ate."

Ron chuckled. "We got leftover sketti or day-old pizza. He can take his pick."

Mary grinned and unmuted the phone. "Ron says sure. I'm glad you're back. Come on over. Have you eaten?"

"Depends on what you call eating. A stale bag of peanuts on the plane. Cold fast-food cheeseburger and a flat soda five hours ago." Jeff's laugh followed. "Ron cooking?"

Mary snickered. "He did if you don't mind leftover sketti, to quote him, or day-old pizza."

"Either sounds great," Jeff answered. "Be there in about forty minutes."

"Ok. See you then." Mary ended the call, glancing at Ron. "Sounds like he'll eat either. I'd wait until he gets here."

Ron nodded, rising and gathering their bowls. "Won't take long to heat either. I'll put another pot of tea on, too."

"Jeff said he liked that peppermint tea you brewed last time. He asked if I knew where you bought it." Mary ran hot water into the opposite sink. She picked up the dishcloth and put it along with her hands into the soapy dishwater.

"Local health food market. They have a wide selection." Ron set their bowls on the counter and faced her. "I need to tell you something."

"Sure. What is it?"

Ron laid his hand on her arm, brushed his lips over hers and said, "I'm falling in love with you."

Chapter Nineteen

"**Y**ou're *what*?" Mary stepped back from the sink, soapsuds and water dripping from her hands onto the floor. She glanced down and back up. "*Shit*. I'm sorry. Let me clean that up."

"I've got it." Ron tossed the dishtowel on the floor, mopping the water up with his foot. "Dry your hands. I'm serious."

Mary took the towel he held out. She kept looking down, intently drying her hands over and over. Any response, any question or prodding he said would come across like he demanded the same in kind. He'd had a few forced declarations of love fail because the other person wasn't there. They cared, they liked him. The hollowness, the empty hours, and the loneliness weren't what he wanted. What he needed. Had he spoke too soon?

Ron started to walk away. Every breath he took stuck in his chest. He couldn't take back what he said. To deny his feelings, what his heart bubbled forth every time he got around Mary, would be lying to himself, to his ego and his heart. He shook out his hands as he got near the kitchen doorway.

"Ron," Mary said from close behind him. "Please wait."

He turned. Mary stood middle of the kitchen, holding her hand out to him.

"I'm waiting." Did he fist his hands, clench them tighter than he had as he walked away? Or shove them into his pockets? Grip them behind his back so he didn't place his heart any firmer in her hands? Was she handing him back his heart and dignity? He wasn't going to change how he felt. Nor could he. Mary held a huge chunk of his heart whether she wanted to or not.

Mary watched Ron's face. Looking for any indication she still had a chance. A possible second chance to say what clobbered her and tossed her deep into her own emotions and heart tugged down into a place she'd been for quite a few weeks. He stared at her, poker-faced. Somber and rigid. She knew he bristled, ready to throw up a wall, safeguarding his heart. She didn't blame him. She'd done the same thing again and again. Ran away from love and the risk. Now she couldn't. Her psyche, mixed with her subconscious needs and desires, echoed what her heart screamed out. Denying herself wasn't an option.

She closed the space between them, speaking as she did. "Thank you."

"For what?" Ron asked, almost in a whisper.

"For loving me. Taking a risk on telling me. Knowing that I might not feel the same way." Mary reached for Ron's hand with both of hers.

Ron shook his head and shoved his hand in his pocket. "I need clarity. What are you saying? Give it to me without any BS."

She moved closer, laid her hand on Ron's forearm. "I care too. What I feel is beyond close friends. More than best buddies as we labeled each other a few months ago."

Ron stepped forward until he stood toe-to-toe with her. He pulled his hand out of his pocket, entwining his fingers with hers. "Do I matter here?" He reached out with his other hand and touched her breast right over her heart.

Mary swallowed, closed her eyes, inhaled, and listened to what her heart responded. She looked up, her gaze meeting Ron's intent one, and said, "Yes. You and your wellbeing are in my thoughts and heart daily."

Ron let go of her hand, slipped both arms around her, hugging her tightly to him. He whispered close to her ear, "It is well. Thank you for caring as much as you do."

Mary pulled back. "You're welcome. I've learned to trust me again. I'm listening to me much better."

Ron tittered. "Oh, yeah. That isn't always easy."

He leaned back toward her with his lips puckered as the doorbell rang. "Damn. Either someone has piss-poor timing or I do." He brushed his lips over hers and stepped away.

Mary snorted. "It's not like we don't know who it is."

"True. But one of us ain't got great timing either way." Ron entered the dining room still talking. "Don't hold it against him. Just need to throw ice water on my lust meter."

"How about both of you don't have good timing?" She followed Ron into the living room and sat on the couch.

"Could be all three of us need to work on our timing," Ron countered, unlocking the door. He glanced back at her, stuck out his tongue, then blew her a kiss and opened the door.

"I am not kissing you," Jeff said, entering the house. "You're not my type."

"Not mine either," Ron answered, closing the door. "That leaves Mary. Are we your type, Mary?"

She pressed her lips together, rolled her eyes heavenward, and fell out laughing. She laughed and laughed until tears started. She looked at Ron, then at Jeff. Both tried to suppress their Cheshire cat grins. Ah, there was no denying it. These two men multiplied the joy in her life. Jeff had never left her heart even though she'd considered breaking up with him. And Ron...well, he'd snuck in like Jeff had just being himself—caring, friendly, and accepting of where she was and who she was when they met. Both had supported her independence and taken an active role in her life. Vast differences from Warren who had nurtured, taken care of her, and most of the time was the family leader. Now, she was independent because she wanted to be and loved it.

"Yes, you're both my type. Maybe I should get those kisses." Mary scooted forward on the couch, her lips puckered.

"Sounds good to me," Jeff said, rounding the couch. He leaned down, rested his hand on Mary's shoulder, and pressed his lips to hers. He traced her bottom lip with his tongue, nibbling at its fullness until she opened her mouth. He entered, tasting her essence, letting her heat mix with his as the mixture slowly enveloped them. Her breath reached out, caressing his face and moving downward, warming him inside and out. She followed him as he retreated as if she didn't want the kiss to end.

Jeff pulled back and glanced at Ron. Ron nodded, gave him a thumbs-up as he approached from the other side. "Since I already got one of those earlier, brief one for me." Ron sat down beside Mary, leaned over, and kissed her cheek. He scooted away, moving toward the opposite end of the couch. "Mary, move closer to me so Jeff has room to sit down."

Mary scooted closer to Ron, patting the space next to her.

"Thanks," Jeff said, sitting down, placing his messenger bag on the floor next to the coffee table. "What you two been up to?"

Ron chuckled. "Talking and dining."

"Yes, spaghetti and meatballs quick and easy with sugar cookies and ice cream for dessert." Mary faced him. "Are you hungry?"

"I can eat. Not right away though." Jeff leaned back into the couch as he kicked off his shoes. "You want to hear a brief on my trip?"

"Yes," Ron said, leaning forward. "Susan called yesterday asking if I would share my rum cake recipe with her chef."

"How did the opening go?" Mary asked.

"Neither Susan, Tim, nor I thought this would take two weeks. Even with a lot of the staffing in place, snags and snafus came up. We pulled it off. I took a turn in the kitchen cooking, too." Jeff reached for his messenger bag.

"Sounds like you were boss and employee at the same time." Mary stood up. She stepped over his feet as he leaned back with his bag in hand. She moved to the chair close to the couch. "Easier to see you both from here."

Jeff nodded. "I helped out cuz the first chef quit on us close to inaugural night. The assistant chef and I carried out prep and a soft lunch opening while Susan interviewed two other chefs."

Ron pointed at the bag. "What's in there?"

Jeff opened the bag, pulled out a folder, and handed it to Ron. "Susan sent recipes we can use at the diner and for the catering business. They're ones she inherited from her grandmother. She kept copies for herself."

Ron leafed through a few of the recipes. "Nice. I'll send her a thank you email in the morning."

Jeff took out another folder. "This one has all my polyamory notes and musings."

"Okay," Ron and Mary said almost at the same time in rather flat tones.

"Not bad stuff," Jeff began taking a page out and laying the folder on the end table next to his end of the couch. "I figured out why I flinched at some of the concepts and rigid rules many felt were needed."

Ron turned so he faced him and Mary. "Some of them sound off, I'm sure."

"It runs counter to being true to what you need and want. I gathered the main aspect of it all is other than basic guidelines we each work out our own rules."

Ron nodded. "Pretty much the same thing I figured out. No two relationships are the same. Different people. Different takes and needs."

"True," Mary chimed in. "You and Ron are alike in some ways. There are unique differences that meet many of my needs. Like Ron taking care of Lindsay and Tabitha. You helped Darcey with a car problem. I like having both of you around and in my life."

"Is this what you wanted to talk about?" Ron asked.

"Part of it." Jeff glanced at the sheet he held. "I journaled one night about my feelings on Mary being with you."

"And?" Mary asked.

"I don't mind it. I know you and trust you. It definitely affected how I saw things even when I was uneasy. I feel more comfortable knowing she's with you than I would if I didn't respect and trust the person. Make sense?"

"Yes. You have a sense of me and my values instead of dealing with unknowns." Ron stood. "Let's continue this in the kitchen while I warm up your food."

Jeff rose, holding his hand out to Mary. She took hold of it, squeezed, and stood. "Sure. Mary, can you get the folder and bring it with you, please?"

He waited until Mary picked up the folder and moved up beside him. He leaned over, kissed her cheek, and whispered, "I love you."

He straightened and walked into the kitchen. He glanced back over his shoulder as he turned toward where Ron stood. Mary hadn't moved. Her lips moved. No words came out. He hesitated, gripped the sheet he held tighter, took a couple of breaths, and left well enough alone. She'd either catch up to them or she'd say something. Communication had to flow both ways. Another thing he learned from his research.

"Mary coming?" Ron asked as he put the spaghetti container on the counter.

"I think so. I thought she was right behind me." Jeff started to move back toward the kitchen doorway.

Ron held up his hand. "Hold on. We were talking before you got here. So she may need a moment."

Jeff sat down at the table. "What were you talking about?"

Ron put part of the leftover spaghetti on a plate and put it in the microwave. As he set the timer, he responded, "Falling in love. What that means and how she feels about it."

"*Fuck.*" Jeff groaned and blew out a deep sigh. "I just told her I love her before I came in here."

"You upset about that?" Ron filled the electric kettle and plugged it in. He sat down next to Jeff. "Wanna take it back?"

"Take back, no. Upset about saying it, no. Wish I had better timing, damn straight on that!"

"First, no one has great timing all the time. Otherwise, we'd never live or get things done." Ron leaned on his elbows on the table. "Two, we aren't responsible for Mary's reaction unless we set out to hurt her."

"Wasn't my plan. I wanted her to know I love her. That I'm okay with this poly thing the three of us are working on." Jeff crumbled the paper he still held.

Ron pried the paper out of Jeff's hand. "Stop feeling sorry for you. You didn't do anything deliberately."

"No," Jeff said, unfisting his hand. "I guess this is one of those more communicate moments."

"Could be. Sometimes you have to let a person assimilate what's been said." Ron smoothed the paper, ran his finger down it, and pointed to an item. "Like your observation here. You aren't always responsible for how people react."

"Easier said than done when you love them." Jeff rocked back, trying to see around him.

"Give her a few more moments. If she hasn't said something by the time your food's ready, we'll check on her." Ron folded the paper in half and slid it across the table to Jeff.

The microwave timer rang. Jeff started to push back from the table as Mary walked into the kitchen. She pulled out the chair on the opposite side of the table and sat down. "Thanks for giving me space. I'm blown away."

Ron put Jeff's plate in front of him, setting utensils and a napkin next to the plate. "How so?"

"Hearing the L word from you both almost at the same time. It's not something that happens every day." Mary rested her chin in her hand as she leaned on the table.

"In poly, you hear it often if both people you're in a relationship with are present. Of course, it's new for you." Ron set two boxes of tea bags on the counter.

"Yes. And I'm still afraid of what if it doesn't work out. What then?"

"Can our friendship and business venture remain intact?" Jeff asked, laying his fork down. He wiped his mouth before he continued. "That worries me, too."

Ron sat down. "There are no guarantees in life. Only what you chose to work on. I'm not afraid to take a chance on us. What about you, Jeff? Mary?"

"I'm with you, Ron," Jeff said, ready to fork more spaghetti into his mouth. "I took the leap before with you, Mary. I loved you then, kept loving you while gone, and fell in love with you now."

"That's what scares me. I can care, cherish, and desire each of you. Risking my heart gives me the willies." Mary chafed her arms.

The kettle started whistling. Ron stood. "Don't you risk every time you do business? Care about someone or something?"

"Isn't risk part of living and loving? At least that's what Ona taught me." Jeff handed his empty plate to him. "Thanks. That was good."

"Welcome. Want tea and cookies, Jeff? Mary?" Ron asked, stepping away from the table.

"Yes. Anything decaf is fine with me," Jeff replied, scooting his chair back from the table. "Mary, why does risking your heart scare you?"

"Ron, tea is fine. Thank you for asking." Mary had tucked her hands into her arms folded tight to her. Ron counted his breaths in and out. His mind tossed questions and replies that were based on his experience. Putting them out there wouldn't do anything to further the conversation. Mary wasn't him.

Ron put Jeff's plate in the sink with the other dishes. He turned around and faced Mary. "Sure. Why are you afraid of loving someone?"

Chapter Twenty

Mary unclenched her fists and slid her arms down until they were at her sides. Letting out this part of her past hadn't come up for a while. She hadn't talked about it with anyone except Sharon. The fear, uncertainty, and loss mixed with learning how to go on and realizing what she didn't know. Apprehension summed up her emotions and lingering concerns. Facing them took more than naming them or admitting she got anxious about taking that risk again. She glanced at Jeff, then to Ron, and spoke.

"Before Warren, I hadn't fallen in love. I cared about people and had a few short-term affairs. But love hadn't come up." She stood, pacing to the counter and back to the table as she continued speaking. "Warren was my first in love experience. We had some difficult times before things smoothed out right before he died."

Ron unplugged the kettle and took three mugs out of the cabinet. He placed a tea bag in each and filled them. He handed two to her as she paced back toward him. She took them and started back toward the table as he spoke. "You're afraid that loving will turn out that way again?"

"Cautious is the word that comes to mind. Possibly overly cautious." Mary set the mugs on the table and sat back down.

Jeff laid his hand on hers. "I think I get it. Your experience isn't overly positive so you're wary that one good time is the freak, right?"

"Yes. I know there's no promises. You and I worked well until you had to leave. I get you had to go."

Ron put the sugar bowl and spoons on the table along with a plate of cookies. "Why did you turn to me?"

Mary blinked, opened her mouth, closed it, and pressed her lips tightly together. Had she turned to Ron? Was she splitting up with Jeff in her mind at that point?

"You know, that is a good question. One that I asked myself when I realized I was attracted to you." Mary added sugar to her tea and stirred. "My honest answer is you attracted me and still do. I want companionship and someone to spend time with."

Ron sat down next to her. "I want the same thing. We get along well and definitely have chemistry." He brushed his lips across her cheek.

Jeff cleared his throat. "Okay, getting used to PDAs is gonna take me some time. I have a request."

Ron handed him a spoon. "What is it?"

"Can we come up with some baseline that works for all of us? Something that defines where we are and where we'd like to go?" Jeff stirred his tea.

"I think this is about going as slow as the slowest needs," Mary offered.

"I can relate to that. I've been there a few times." Ron sugared his tea and stirred it. "Mary, you seem to have a squick or two happening."

"Squick? What's that?" She glanced at Jeff, noting his puzzled look. "Looks like Jeff wants to know, too."

"That's one word I didn't come across." Jeff patted the folder she'd laid on the table. "Damn, no pen."

"I'll get one. Keep them with the grocery list pad." Ron stood, walked over to the counter, talking as he opened a drawer. "Squick is a word BDSMers use. It's similar to pluck nerve or knee jerk. Something bothers you."

Mary nodded. "I'll be honest, hearing *I love you* from both of you pushed a button or two."

"How so?" Ron asked, sitting back down.

"It felt like I'm a prize both of you were competing for. I know you're not since neither of you knew the other had said it until a few minutes ago."

Jeff set his mug down, sighing. "What am I supposed to do?"

Mary reached over, took Jeff's hand, and squeezed it. "You did nothing wrong. You said what your heart guided you to say. It's my reaction."

Ron cleared his throat. "Is this the first you had someone take a serious interest in you since Warren?"

Mary nodded again. "Yes," she said, looking down. "Jeff started showing signs of stronger interest before going to Europe."

She tipped her head back, brushing her hair off her face with her free hand. She reached for Ron's hand. He cupped both of his around hers. She glanced at Jeff and back to Ron. Wetting her lips, she added, "I'm scared and happy at the same time. I gave both of you a large piece of my heart."

"Are you saying you love us?" Jeff asked, brushing his lips over the back of her hand.

"I-I think so." Mary stared at Ron, wanting to know how he felt with her unobtrusive declaration.

Ron let go of Mary's hand. Scooting his chair back and standing, he moved behind her, leaned down, wrapped both arms around her shoulders, and hugged her. "Thank you. It's good to know your feelings."

Ron let go and turned to Jeff, holding out a hand. "Let's shake on this."

"Why?" Jeff asked, taking hold of his hand.

"Verbal and symbolic agreement that we're in this together." Ron gave Jeff a firm handshake, let go, and sat down.

"Some couples and triads write up a formal agreement." Jeff pulled the folder to him. He opened it, leafing through the sheets inside.

Ron tapped on the table, glancing at Mary and Jeff. "I know about those. Some need rigid rules and expectations. Others want a framework to guide them with boundaries spelled out."

"Seems like a lot of back and forth that maybe we aren't ready for?" Mary nudged Jeff, scooting her chair closer to him. "Are you wanting a fence to keep you in or others out?"

Jeff sighed, shutting the folder. He laid his hands on top of it. "Is this where we start to define us? This is the no man's land some say is the tricky part?"

Ron snorted, leaning back in his chair. "Depends on your perspective. I know I want some guidelines. Call it a foundation. What about you, Mary?"

"I want us to get along and stay friends. What basics do we want as guidelines?" Mary pulled Jeff's folder out from under his hands. "Got a clean sheet in there?" She reached for the pen Ron had put on the table.

"Yes, at the bottom of the stack." Jeff pushed the pen to Mary. "I want...no, I need no competition. No others lurking or trying to get in with us."

"Not a bad base rule. I feel the same way when I start new relationships." Ron pointed at Mary. "I think that's our first rule."

Mary nodded. "Rule number one. No additions or other relationships at this time." She drummed the pen against the table and asked, "What about family and their relationships?"

"This pertains to adding to the three of us. We'll discuss family blood and extended as a unit." Jeff leaned forward. "That way none of us gets blindsided."

"Okay, no adding to us. Family isn't part of the no addition rule." Mary wrote down the addendum. "What else?"

"If something affects the three of us, we talk it out. No making one-sided decisions for the trio." Ron stood and moved his chair around the table closer to Mary so he could see the paper as she wrote.

"Good point," Jeff added. "Couple time is a must. It allows dates and privacy for..." His voice trailed off. He looked up. "Well, you know what I mean."

"Sex?" Mary offered.

"Love making?" Ron countered. "After all, we've used and said love a few times this evening."

Jeff pulled the paper to him. "I think we need to get some basic things written down first, then go from there."

"Yes," Ron said, tapping the sheet. "We need to agree on what goes on here. This is about three, not just one or two."

Mary nodded, writing down couple time and dates. "All right. What else?"

"Trio dates? Time for the three of us to relax together?" Jeff sat back, smiling. "We've got a business to talk about, too."

Ron nodded. "Sure do. That is separate from this."

Mary grinned. "I got one more item I think we all agree on. No business discussions on date nights."

"Oh, yeah, "Ron said. "That could ruin downtime. We want time to relax for sure."

"I agree." Jeff pointed to the sheet. "Nice addition, Mary."

"Thank you."

"Do we want to spell out overnights?" Jeff asked.

"How about that is part of couple date nights as wanted?" Ron turned his chair sideways. "I'm cool with it as long as we know overnight is part of it."

Jeff nodded. "Yes, that way we aren't caught off-guard. Better knowing than not."

Mary laid the pen down. "I think we've got a good basis to work with."

"Agreed," Ron said.

"Same with me." Jeff said.

Ron reached for the pen. "Let me add a couple of things real quick." He pulled the sheet to him.

"Like what?" Jeff asked, standing and leaning over Mary to see what he was doing.

"Hold on. I'll show you in a moment." Ron wrote things at the top of the paper and added several lines to the bottom of the list. He turned the paper toward Jeff and Mary.

Mary looked up, smiling. "Nice. I like."

Jeff pulled the sheet to him, running his finger up and down the page. He grinned as he held the sheet up. "Great job, Ron."

Ron took the sheet back from Jeff. "I'll sign it first, okay?"

"How about some verbal and symbol like you and Jeff did between us?" Mary asked.

"I like that," Jeff said. "Makes it kinda formal."

Ron chuckled. "As formal as we can get."

Mary took hold of his hand, reaching for Jeff's with her other. "Let's hold hands. Jeff, you take Ron's, please."

"Sure." Jeff took hold of his hand.

The three of them sat silently for several moments, looking at each other. Ron spoke first. "Mary, you said you thought you loved us earlier. How are you feeling now?"

Mary raised his hand to her lips, kissing the back of his hand, doing the same with Jeff's. She held both close to her heart as she said, "I believe in our love. Our commitment to our family and us. I love you both."

"Me too," Jeff said, squeezing his hand.

"As do I." Ron squeezed Jeff and Mary's hands.

Ron let go of Jeff and Mary's hands. "Now, back to signing this paper. I printed our names at the top like we're taking a vow. At the bottom, we sign and date. What do you think?"

Jeff reached for the pen as Mary let go of his hand. "I'm on board. I'll sign."

"I'm ready to sign, too." Mary slid the sheet to Jeff. "Here's the pen."

"Thanks." Jeff printed his name in one of the spaces Ron made. He signed the bottom and dated it. He handed the pen to Mary.

"I'll take the middle space." Mary printed her name, signed the corresponding area below, and turned to Ron. "Your turn."

"Great." Ron added his name and signature to the paper. He retrieved his tea mug, held it up, and said, "Here's to us. A family full of love, promise, and a future built together."

"Here. Here," Jeff and Mary added, clinking their mugs with his.

Ron moved around the table until he stood behind Mary and Jeff. He held out both hands. "How about our first family hug?"

Mary stood up and moved next to him. She slid her arm around his waist, motioning Jeff to her. Jeff joined them, sliding an arm around Mary and his other around him. They closed the space until they hugged each other tightly.

Mary pressed her lips together, glancing at Ron and Jeff. She wasn't a weak-kneed person, yet an overwhelming urge to sit down with Ron and Jeff cuddling her between them filled her. She didn't want to let go of either. Part of her felt like if she did let go and stopped touching either of them, she'd wake up, and all this would be a dream.

Ron laid his hand on her shoulder. He softly squeezed her shoulder as he spoke. "Is something wrong? Jeff and I are here because we want to be. Telling us what you want or need is all part of this."

"Just so much caring, compassion, and love all at once is a bit overwhelming." Mary blinked again. One tear, then another, streamed down her cheeks. She sighed deeply and added, "I need to sit down. All of a sudden I'm weak in the knees."

Jeff reached down, took hold of the hem of his t-shirt, and used it to wipe the tears off her cheek closest to him. "I think sitting down is a good idea. I'm getting a bit wobbly, too."

Ron let go of her shoulder, slid his other arm around her, and walked over to the counter. He picked up the paper towel roll, speaking as he moved back to her and Jeff. "One of the reasons I have a large couch. Three-person cuddle size is a must."

Ron took her hand, the roll of paper towels in his other, and started toward the living room. Jeff followed her, still holding her hand.

Ron set the paper towels on the coffee table, pulled the table back some from the couch, and sat down. He patted the space next to him. "Mary, cuddle right up to me. That leaves room for Jeff right next to you."

Mary sat next to him, scooting close enough that they touched. Ron put his arm around her shoulders. Jeff sat on the other side of Mary. He took hold of her hand. Ron leaned forward, pointing to Jeff. "It's okay to put your arm around her. Our touching is fine. That's part of this, too. You and I know there's a limit to the sensual touch we share."

Jeff nodded. "Right. I don't want to mess up."

"Know that feeling real well. Did that a few times myself. I learned compersion plays a large part in this." Ron leaned back.

"Compersion?" Jeff asked.

"That's being joyful because someone you care about is joyful, right?" Mary asked.

"Yes, we're all experiencing each other's joy. Contagious joy multiplied by another's joy." Ron took his arm down from around Mary's shoulders. He turned catty-cornered on the couch, leaning against the arm. "Jeff, what is it about our touching that bothers you?"

"I've got to let go of the idea touching you means I'm sexually attracted to you. Or vice versa." Jeff rose and sat on the coffee table. "I know you're not. It's internalizing it."

"Trust is the root. Letting go and trusting is part of this, too. How about you, Mary?"

"I'm anxious I won't speak up due to fear, or I'll panic either of you off."

Jeff held up his hand. "I think we're focusing on negatives here instead of the joy. How about we change topic?"

"Go ahead," Ron encouraged.

"Sure," Mary said.

"What are we curious about with this? What are things we want to try? Make us feel good?" Jeff asked.

"I like that," Ron said, standing up. "I feel joy when I see my love feeling joy and love."

Mary squirmed. Jeff laid his hand on Mary's arm. "What's wrong?"

Mary shook her head. Ron scooted closer to her. Jeff dropped to his knees in front of her.

Ron spoke first. "Something's bothering you. We need to know what it is. We want to know what it is."

"He's right. Please tell us what's going on here and here." Jeff touched her heart and gut.

Mary exhaled, her lips pressed together. Her heart's steady rhythm spoke loudly. Her jittery stomach flip-flopped much less than when the discussion began. She took ahold of Ron's hand, then Jeff's hand. She wet her lips, closed her eyes, and said the words that intrigued and worried her. "Getting used to being affectionate with both of you at the same time. Cuddling like this is helping some."

She opened her eyes and glanced at her hands. Jeff and Ron hadn't let go. She looked up first at Ron and then Jeff. Neither frowned nor scowled. Both of them wore the same expression. Eyes open gazing at her with a soft smile and relaxed posture. She opened her mouth, sucked in air, and let go of a soft sigh.

"Babe," Jeff said, holding her hand between his. "Are you saying you want this?"

"Yes. I'm afraid you and Ron don't want it."

Ron laid his head on Mary's shoulder. "Don't worry about what all the vids show. Or the hype on it from your research. We do what we want, okay?"

"That works for me." Mary let go of his hand and patted his cheek.

"Me too," Jeff said, standing up.

"How about we try this from a different perspective?" Ron offered.

"What you got in mind?" Jeff bent over, touching his toes, and straightened back up. He put his hands on his hips, bending back as far as he could before righting himself.

Ron stood and stretched also. "Stretched out on my king-sized bed."

Chapter Twenty-One

"That does level the playing field." Jeff held one hand out to Mary and his other to Ron. "Comfort physically and emotionally matter."

Mary loosely placed her hand in his. Jeff glanced at Mary. She smiled and looked away. Ron was walking toward the stairs. "Hang on, Ron."

Jeff moved in front of Mary, speaking as he did. "Mary, are you all right?"

Mary looked at him, nodding. She pointed to the stairs. "Yes. I'm ready to take this to the next level up there."

Jeff walked to the stairs. Facing Ron, he said, "Ladies first."

Ron nodded. "Yes, ladies first."

Mary swallowed hard. They faced her, holding out their hands. Her next move could make or break what happened next. Was she in, or did everything stop here?

She walked around the coffee table and didn't stop until she reached the base of the stairs. She leaned over kissed Jeff and then Ron. Without looking back, she took the stairs two at a time.

Ron looked at Jeff, who shrugged, grinning. "I think that's an unspoken yes."

Ron snorted. "I do believe so. Let's not keep our lady waiting." He trotted up the stairs. Jeff following closely behind him.

Mary continued down the hall, stopping outside Ron's bedroom door. She'd caught what Jeff and Ron said as she reached the top of the stairs. They were right about it being an unspoken yes. What it entailed, she wasn't sure yet. Their discussion got her thinking and wondering how much she and Warren could have done differently to enrich their marriage. Love hadn't come into play until shortly before Warren's death. How was she going to make this time not the same? She took a deep breath, held it, and exhaled. This time she was asking for what she wanted and needed by being an active partner.

"Guys," Mary called out. "What's the holdup?"

Ron reached the top of the stairs as he answered, "Nothing that waiting isn't improving."

Jeff stopped behind Ron. "Yeah, what he said."

Ron followed Mary partway into his bedroom. Evidence of their earlier lovemaking wasn't present. He hadn't known why at the time the need to tidy up hit him strongly. Now he did. It was like getting into someone's used bathwater. Everything about it reeked of cast-off, not good enough. Starting out with a level feeling allowed for comfort and unity instead of one-upmanship. None of them needed that. He paused at the door, ensuring Jeff followed. "Come on in, dude. We're all welcome."

Jeff halted as he reached the bedroom door. This was Ron's domain. He'd been here before as a friend seeing the house after Ron had bought and decorated. This time he was entering as someone different. Once he stepped into the room, things changed. Their friendship went to another level that wasn't lovers or friends with benefits as some would label them. They were triad partners. How he'd define or explain that still needed smoothing out. He'd come this far; he wasn't backing out now. Fear no longer drove him. He was in control. He spoke as he entered the room. "Yes, we're all welcome. Thanks for the invitation."

Mary took hold of Jeff's hand as he entered. She knew what it was like to feel like a third wheel, left out and isolated. She held out her other hand to Ron. "I need another hug."

Ron entwined his fingers with her, moving closer. Jeff let go of her hand and slid his arm around her waist, snuggling to her. Each moved tighter to her until they touched toe-to-toe, legs close together and bodies hugging each other. Ron and Jeff's breaths mingled with hers, enveloping them in their own sphere of caring and desire. Mary tilted her head back, allowing her to see Jeff and Ron clearly. She closed her eyes and focused on what each beat of her heart told her. "I want to cuddle nude with you both."

Ron brushed his lips over Mary's. He moved back until he could easily see Jeff and Mary. Their gazes met his. He stepped back further until the back of his legs touched the bed. Ron pulled his shirt over his head and dropped it on the floor. "I think we've got too many clothes on."

"I agree," Jeff said, moving away from Mary until he stood near the bed facing Mary. He took hold of the hem of his t-shirt, slowly pulling it up, exposing the end of the hairline V thrusting deep down beyond the waistbands of his shorts and briefs. He continued pulling upward revealing his abs and finally his chest. Over his head and onto the floor next to Ron's shirt his went. He pointed to Ron and himself, asking, "Like the view?"

Mary nodded and grabbed the hem of her top. She yanked it over her head and tossed it as close as she could to the guys' shirts. "I like the view."

She moved closer to Ron and Jeff, reaching for her bra clasp as she did. Stepping between both of them, she glanced at each, winked and sat on the foot of the bed.

Ron sat on her left. Jeff on her right. Slipping their arms around her, they placed a hand on her stomach slightly above the button and zipper of her shorts. Jeff leaned in, brushing his lips over hers once, twice, three times. On the third time, he pressed his partially opened lips to hers. Ron kissed her shoulder, laving his way up to her neck, nibbling where her neck and shoulder met until he clasped her earlobe between his lips, suckling and softly biting it.

Jeff began tracing her lips with the tip of his tongue. His hand swept upward across her back until his fingers tangled in her hair as he cupped her head. He pressed his lips firmer to hers, seeking entrance. Mary opened her mouth, ready to savor every sip and taste he offered.

Ron let go of her earlobe and whispered hotly against her ear, "I'm getting hot watching you and Jeff."

Jeff broke off the kiss. He rested his forehead against hers, turned his head slightly, and said, "Knowing you're watching is turning me on. How you doing, Mary?"

"Oh yes, it's very hot in here." Mary fanned herself, blinking as Jeff pulled further back. "It's like I stepped outside myself and watched from across the room."

"Let's keep increasing the temperature," Jeff offered, leaning back and undoing the button of his shorts. He worked the zipper down until more of the apex of his hairline V showed, along with the top of his briefs. He leaned back farther until he rested on his elbows on the bed. "Ron?"

"Heat keeps rising." Ron stood, unbuttoned his jeans, and slid the zipper part way down. He sat down on the bed close to Mary. "Your turn, darlin.'"

Mary shrugged, sending one bra strap cascading part way down her right arm. As she started to reach for it, Ron took hold of her hand. "Honey, I think you can use some help. Jeff, the other strap, please."

"My pleasure—no, our pleasure." Jeff sat up, hooked his finger in the bra strap on her left shoulder. "On the count of three, shall we?"

"One...two...three," Ron said, slipping the strap he held down her arm and over her hand. Mary started to reach up with one hand to keep her bra from falling.

"No, no," Jeff said, quickly sliding her other strap down and off her arm and hand. "Bare-chested is equal opportunity."

Jeff tugged her bra from under her hand, exposing her left breast. He raised his head and kissed her.

As he pulled back, Jeff noted the constraints of his briefs and shorts, pulling tight against the crack of his ass, pulled them even tighter around his balls. How much more could either take before he outright shucked them, he didn't know. He glanced at Ron, who watched him and Mary intently. Jeff laid his free hand between Mary's breasts. "This side is bare. What about yours?"

Ron picked up Mary's hand, pulled her bra completely off, and tossed it on the floor. He cupped her breast lightly, pressing upward until his hand was level with Jeff's full one. "Both sides are bare. Equal opportunity bare chests."

Mary tried to take a deep breath. Heat and need coursed through her hotter than any hundred-degree day during a Santa Ana wind blowing up from the southern California deserts. "I could use some water. It's warm in here."

"Chemistry will do that." Ron rose. "I'll get you some water."

Jeff slipped his arm around Mary's shoulders and hugged her to him. "You okay? If we need to stop, let us know."

Ron handed Mary a cup of water. Mary drank the water and handed Ron the empty cup. She turned in Jeff's arm until she faced him. "I'm fine. Outside my comfort zone."

"We all are at some point," Ron added.

Jeff glanced from her to Ron and back. "You learn something new every day."

"You often do." Ron crumpled the paper cup and tossed it in the bedside trashcan. He unzipped his jeans, grabbed the waistbands of his jeans and boxers, and shoved them down his legs. He stepped out of his boxers and jeans, kicking them aside.

He sat down on the bed, leaned back until he lay flat, and rolled on his side. "It's a hell of a lot more comfortable. Why don't you get comfortable?"

Mary glanced at him, arching an eyebrow. He grinned and vigorously nodded. "Yup, naked-nude-bare assed. Whatever you call it, why not do it?"

Jeff chuckled, got up, and stood in front of them. "I'm tired of my briefs and shorts invading the crack of my ass," he said, undoing the zipper completely and hooking his thumbs in the waistband of both. He pushed them off, kicking them away from him. He sat close to Mary and said, "That leaves you, sweetie. You gonna or not?"

Mary looked over her shoulder at Ron, who lay on his side, propped up by one elbow. Each watched her, waiting for her to take off her panties, her last piece of clothing, her signal she was in for what came next. She exhaled slowly, rose, and walked a short distance away from the bed. "I love seeing both of you nude."

Ron and Jeff nodded and pointed at her. Jeff spoke first. "Your turn for show and tell." He patted the space between Ron and him.

Ron patted the space, too, and added, "Take it off, darlin'."

Mary took hold of the waistband of her panties and turned around. She worked them down and off one hip, wiggled her hips from side to side, and pulled her panties off her other hip. Down her thighs until they reached her knees, she left them fall, loosely holding on to them. She spread her feet and let go of her panties. She lifted one foot out of her panties, then her other. She kicked them aside.

"Nice," Jeff said, moving off the bed. He walked around her. He offered her one of his hands and pulled her into his arms, pressing his lips to hers. He traced her lips with his tongue, opening his mouth more as he retraced her bottom lip. Mary opened her mouth, giving him entrance. She moved tighter to him until they had a full body press going on. Jeff tangled his hand in her hair, tugging lightly. He pulled his tongue back. She gave chase, pressing even tighter to him.

Warmth covered her back as Ron hugged her from behind.

Ron noticed the look on Jeff's face. Ron sat down facing Jeff and Mary. "Something got you squicked, Jeff?"

Jeff didn't respond for several moments. If his furrowed brow and pouting lips indicated where his thoughts went, the cuddle might have died before it went any further. Ron stood, ready to call things a failed attempt.

"Wait," Mary called out, grasping his arm. "This isn't about competition. We're all in or we're all out. I want to go ahead."

Jeff looked up, reaching for Mary's hand. "Are you sure?"

Silence welled up until its pregnant presence threatened to burst like a ruptured balloon. Mary moved away from Jeff, stood, and walked across the room until she reached the window. She pulled back the curtain, looking outside. She inhaled, held her breath, and glanced back at Ron, who shrugged and folded his arms tight against his chest. She exhaled and looked at Jeff, who kept glancing from Ron to her. Letting go of the curtain, she faced the bed and voiced her decision. "Yes, I want to go ahead. If we give up without trying, then we'll never know."

"Never know what?" Ron asked as she moved closer to him.

"Know if we can do it. Know if we like it. If I like it. And..." She held her hands out palms up to Ron and Jeff.

"And?" Jeff asked, leaning toward her, reaching for her hand again.

"And how we're going to work together in pleasure and struggles. It takes the three of us to do this. It's not just one or two." Mary took Jeff's hand, squeezed it, and looked at Ron.

He nodded, taking her hand, giving hers a reassuring squeeze. "Yes, we're all in or it doesn't work. I'm game to keep on going if we're all in."

Jeff stood, still holding her hand. He moved closer to Ron, holding out his hand to him. "I'm admitting I'm in new experience territory. If I fumble, coach me, please, cuz I'm in."

Ron took Jeff's hand and closed the circle. "We'll coach each other. Mutual pleasure is the goal."

He squeezed Mary and Jeff's hands and let go. Moving closer to Mary, he continued speaking. "Positions are important. Jeff, we're going to touch each other a lot. You cool with that?"

Jeff looked down, back up, and dropped Mary's hand. He faced Ron. "Trust is a part of this."

"Yes, it is."

"We've worked in small kitchens together. Shared tight living quarters when things were tough for both of us. I learned then as I believe now. You're trustworthy. I'm cool with touching."

Ron walked over to him and slipped his arm around his waist, giving him a side hug. He smiled as he turned back toward Mary. "Thank you. I trust you, too. If any of us needs to slow down or stop, we say so. That good for everyone?"

Mary nodded, sitting down on the bed. "Yes. I trust both of you, too."

Jeff hugged Ron and stepped away. "What happens now?"

"Logistics, I think. Talk position before we do much more." Ron sat down next to Mary.

"Agreed," Jeff replied, sitting cross-legged on the bed close to Mary. "What's your suggestion?"

"Mary, what do you think about side-by-side?" Ron asked.

"It might work."

"How are we all going to fit together?" Jeff asked.

"Yes. Mary lays on her side. I'm behind her. You're in front."

"Sounds doable," Jeff offered. He kneeled on the bed. Ron's gaze met his.

Ron stretched out behind Mary, spooning to her. Mary's gaze met his as he slid his arm around her waist, hugging her briefly.

"Jeff, I'm ready for your part of my hug." Mary patted the space close to her.

Jeff laid on his side, scooting closer to Mary. As he reached her, Ron's gaze met his. Ron winked, smiled and nodded. Jeff inhaled as he slowly exhaled he cuddled tight to Mary, laying his arm on her waist, touching Ron. Mary brushed her lips over his, turned her head slightly and briefly kissed Ron.

Quiet filled the room. This time without angst or fear inflating it. The three of them lay cocooned together. Several delicious moments passed as they lay entwined, dozing.

Ron blinked, inhaled deeply, and exhaled slowly. Jeff lay tight to Mary, his forehead resting on her shoulder. Mary stroked his head with one hand.

Ron rolled onto his back and sat up. They'd done it. Had a three-way nude cuddle. Even napped together. A great first time.

"Thanks," Jeff said, sitting up.

"For what?" Ron asked.

"A new experience."

"You're welcome," Ron said as he dressed.

"One more thing," Jeff said.

"Yeah?"

"I'm glad we're in this together."

Ron paused by the bed as Mary sat up and scooted to the edge of the bed. "How you doing?"

Mary smiled and motioned him closer. He stopped a few inches from the bed, holding his hand out. She shook her head, rose, and moved closer until she stood toe-to-toe with him. Mary looped her arms around his neck and pressed her lips to his.

Jeff and Mary sat beside each other, smiling as they put their clothes on.

Ron grinned, knowing that they'd grown closer. What came next, he didn't know. He knew Mary had taken a chance. Jeff, too. All of them had dared to risk their hearts and let love in again. Whatever their future brought, they would face it together because love united them.

Epilogue

T *en Months Later*

"Happy anniversary," Mary called out, entering the dining room. She carried a cake with three lit candles on the tray.

"Anniversary? Already?" Jeff asked, pulling aside the chair she'd sat in.

"We hadn't set a date that I know of," Ron added, taking the tray from her.

"Why not now?" Mary asked. "Our business is doing well. We signed the contract for the new combined office space. Even our attorney and accountant gave us thumbs up on the expansion."

"How about we blow out the candles?"

"On three."

"One."

"Two."

"Three." They blew together, extinguishing the flames.

"And we're doing great," Jeff offered, pulling the candles out of the cake. "Ona can't stop talking about her visit each time we talk. She loves how thriving we are. She even said Dad would be proud of me."

"Nana Rose keeps telling me I take after Grandpa Jack." Ron handed Mary a plate as she sliced the cake.

"Each of you explain, please." She put a piece of cake on the plate and pointed to Jeff. "You go first."

"Dad and Ona had an open marriage. They had other lovers from time to time. They went through rough patches, figuring it all out like we have. Their commitment to family and each other helped them come through it all."

Ron took the last plate from Mary. "Nana Rose told Abebi and me she and Grandpa Jack lived together before they married. Even had a few flings before and after they tied the knot. I guess Abebi and I come by our polyness naturally."

Mary held up her fork. "Well, Darcey admitted to me she's moving closer to Jaxson and Nathan. They're spending a lot of time together."

"Abebi's relationship with Jess and Mack is moving along nicely, too." Ron held out his fork. "Here's to love and being together."

Mary touched her fork to Ron's and Jeff's. She gazed at Ron and Jeff as they began eating their cake. She'd risked her heart. Dared to love again. And found love that returned twofold. The risk and dare were definitely worth it.

Whatever the future held, they'd face it together, knowing they had each other to lean on and support them.

THE END

Don't miss out!

Visit the website below and you can sign up to receive emails whenever Solara Gordon publishes a new book. There's no charge and no obligation.

https://books2read.com/r/B-A-RAUJ-YPLZB

BOOKS 2 READ

Connecting independent readers to independent writers.

Did you love *Love's Triple Play*? Then you should read *Caught by Love's Slow Burn*[1] by Solara Gordon!

[2]

Peyton Corners' new fire station commander Brent Stephens is unsure of his growing interest in Bunny Kater. If he could keep his internal smoke detector from going off every time he gets near Bunny, he might be able to understand why she affects like she does.

Bunny Kater has sworn off firemen and intimacy until she meets Brent. Brent unexpectedly awakens her isolated emotions. As she approaches her fortieth birthday, she's trying to figure out why a younger man is interested in her.

Second chances happen one chance at a time, but neither Brent nor Bunny is sure they're going to get a first one.

Read more at https://solaragordon.com/.

---

1. https://books2read.com/u/mZZp6R

2. https://books2read.com/u/mZZp6R

Also by Solara Gordon

Watch for more at https://solaragordon.com/.

About the Author

Solara loves and lives with her partner of 21 years in the Metro DC area. What started out as a bi-coastal romance soon settled on one coast.

A vivid imagination keeps her busy creating her next fascinating romance. She enjoys creating unique characters and watching their journeys unfold. "Love freely given multiplies and will return endlessly" is a key aspect of her stories. Add in alternative lifestyles and her love for the paranormal, and the uncommon becomes the norm in many of her stories.

Her day job in the financial services industry pays the bills while she pens her erotic tales.

Read more at https://solaragordon.com/.

www.ingramcontent.com/pod-product-compliance
Lightning Source LLC
Chambersburg PA
CBHW070311040726
47501CB00019B/2263